Tens A Crowd part five; - Into

When you left us at the end of part

out we were pregnant. It was our first anniversary and we were extremely happy. Not to mention scared and excited. Both of us had more than adequate amounts of first-hand experience with babies and children. I already had more nephews and nieces than I had fingers. Patricia's big sister Betty with her four children was doing her best to keep pace with my oldest brother Donnie and his wife Annie, with their five children. So between us we had 15 nephews and nieces, 16 if you counted Daisy, who had tragically died when I was younger.

Being parents should have been a walk in the park for us, in theory.

Chapter twenty five; Buddy can you spare a dime.

'Where are you going Danny, come on lie down and hold me, I'm a wee bit scared' Patricia said catching the tail of my t-shirt as I tried to get out of bed.

'I want to phone Charlie and my ma' I said, giving in to her tugging at me and lying back down beside her. I immediately lifted her shirt; I couldn't keep my hands away from her extremely flat and immaculately smooth belly.

'Scared about what, don't be daft. He's in there right now, my wee boy, he is only a wee tadpole but he's in there and I bet he can hear me" I said putting my lips to her belly and whispering into it.

'Why Charlie' she asked.

'Why Charlie what?' I answered, playing for time.

‘You said you want to phone Charlie and your ma, but you said Charlie first. So why Charlie” she asked, pulling my hair and turning my head around so I was looking at her and not her belly.

‘Did I?” I asked innocently.

‘You know you did Danny. For god’s sake this isn’t going to be a competition between you two is it? My boys bigger than your boy, my boy runs faster than your boy and all that nonsense, tell me it isnae going to be like that Danny.’ She said in a tone that let me know this wasn’t a request. Not by any manner of means.

‘No. I’m all excited, am I not allowed to be excited. You are having a wean. Our wean, our wee boy’ I said successfully changing the subject.

‘Or lassie’ she said and pulled me up closer to her and kissed me. ‘Don’t you go and set your heart on a boy and then be disappointed if it’s a lassie’ she said.

‘Don’t be daft baby’ I said kissing her back ‘It’s a boy, you know and I know it. It’s a boy’ I said kissing her belly again and getting carried away as usual. ‘I think I can remember the night you got pregnant and I told you right there and then that you were up the duff and that it was a boy’

She laughed and said ‘So you did, I can remember that as well it was about six weeks ago and I told you to shut it and don’t be stupid’ She said looking at me with suspicion.

‘I told you when I met you that I was part gypsy. I can see your future and it involves a lot of this’ I said in what I imagined was a gypsy voice and started groping her.

'What is wrong with you, you're like one of them wee randy dogs that tries to do it with everybody's legs, get off me and go and do what you were gonnae do' she said laughing and pushing me off the bed.

I did phone Charlie first, not for the reasons Patricia thought. I would never encourage competition between any of my nephews and nieces and any of my children. They would all be like brothers and sisters rather than cousins, as far as I was concerned. It was the McCallister's against everybody else, no question. I might fight Charlie every day for the rest of my life. But our children wouldn't be like us, we would both make sure of that.

He seemed to be as stupidly happy as I was. The same as I was when he told me about Iris being pregnant the year before, I had went drinking with him that night and couldn't have been happier if it was me that was going to be a father. We got the jail that night of course, and the night that Iris gave birth to wee Charlie. Come to think of it maybe it was about time we got the jail because of me, rather than him.

'Were you deliberately trying to get us huckled tonight Danny' It was Charlie's voice I could hear him but I couldn't see him.

'Where are you Charlie, in fact where are we, and how can I not see anything' I shouted.

'Thanks to you kissing that polis woman and then trying to head butt her big mate, we are in Partick polis office' he shouted back. A shouting voice came from farther away.

'Will you two shut the fuck up' it said, in a less than friendly tone.

‘Why don’t you make us, you fanny’ Charlie shouted back and then shouted in a slightly different voice ‘Danny don’t shout at that poor man he is only trying to do his job’

I laughed to myself, even if the guy came down and set about me, he would be hard pushed to make me feel worse than I already did. ‘Charlie I canny see. I think I might have gone blind, what were we drinking?” I asked trying to rub some vision into my eyes; I was pressing the heels of both hands into my eyes with no result.

‘I was drinking diesel, the last round I got you were drinking babysham” he said half giggling.

‘No I wisnae you fanny, I’m serious I can hardly see a bloody thing, you’re not funny. I might be blind you dickhead.” I said starting to see shades of light and dark.

‘It’s not even four o’clock yet, it’s dark outside you eejit. And if your eyes are sore it’s either because you were rubbing them all night because you have been greeting the whole time about going to be a daddy. Or it’s because that fat bird that tried to chat you up in Baxter’s threw half a pint of cider in your face when you told her she was incredibly ugly’

‘And then asked her why she thought that you would ever consider humping her when the most beautiful woman in Scotland was waiting up the road for you to go home. By the way does Patricia know that she’s only the most beautiful woman in Scotland now? When you first met her, you told me she was the most beautiful woman in the world. What’s next Danny boy? That’s a slippery slope brother, in a couple of years she will only be the most beautiful woman in your close.’ He said and started braying with laughter like a demented donkey.

I was almost starting to remember some things and come to think of it my eyes were all sticky. I picked at my eyelashes and realised that they were glued together, that's why I couldn't see a thing.

"What was that fat bird drinking, cider and Evo-Stik, my eyelids are glued down and itching like mad" I shouted at stupid arse. Charlie that is, not the turnkey.

"I got her pint of diesel, the same as me" he said giggling again.

For the uninitiated diesel is a concoction made up of half a pint of lager, half a pint of cider and a large dash of Ribena or any other cheaper blackcurrant cordial.

'No wonder I canny see, that pish you drink has welded my eyes shut, and by the way, purely for your information, Patricia is and will always be the most beautiful woman in the universe. But if I wasn't with her I wouldn't kick Iris out of bed on a cold Sunday morning, before the papers got delivered.' I said and it was my turn to bray with laughter. He went quiet, very quiet, I had made a mistake.

'Do you want to repeat that Danny' he asked, very politely.

'I'm sorry Charlie, it was a wee joke. Okay? I am sorry' I said with genuine remorse. Charlie had a tendency towards jealousy. What am I saying? Telling you that Charlie was jealous was like telling you that the Sun was burny. All the McCallister's have a jealous streak male and female. But Charlie takes it to extremes; he's quite possibly the only man in the world that is worse than me for jealousy.

"Charlie" I shouted.

“I’m going to sleep Danny, I might get two hours before they take us to the Sherriff court, what is it you want, it better be good” Charlie answered me wearily.

“Did I tell you I’m going to be a da, Patricia’s having a baby” I said.

“You told me, well done, now go to fucking sleep” he said with genuine pleasure in his voice.

It didn’t turn out as bad as it could have; the desk sergeant dropped the police assault charges. Mainly because had a good laugh at the thought of me trying to head butt the constable who arrested me, he was six foot five. We did get done with drunk and disorderly and we both got twenty pound fines, Charlie paid them on the spot. Charlie must also have paid for most if not all of the drink as well. I had gone out with fifteen quid in my pocket, fifteen quid I couldn’t really afford to spend on drink. But I got home with eighteen quid in my pocket. So either we went to the cheapest pubs in the world or Charlie done the honours as usual.

As the mists of drunkenness cleared in the morning, I remembered Charlie and me bumping into Donnie and Dunky in the Old Toll bar during our I’m-going-to-be-a-daddy pub crawl. Dunky as usual had hugged me and shook my hand and slipped some money into it, Donnie also as usual had shook my hand but didn’t bother with the money part. Dunky had slipped me about thirty quid which explained my relative wealth. When I did eventually get home, Patricia didn’t exactly go ballistic but it was close. Apparently when the police asked me if I wanted anybody informed of my whereabouts, I told them to let my ma know. Oops.

I was still working part time hours at the bookies, but the owner had reduced me to a Saturday shift only. Apparently even he was struggling to make ends meet. He claimed that because of the high number of unemployed good-for-nothings that Maggie Thatcher had created that he was as skint as any ordinary punter. He told me all this while hanging his elbow out of the driver's side window of his jag. I mentioned that his bookies shop benefited from high unemployment, because there were three times as many punters in there every day as their used to be.

He said 'That type aren't spending money Danny, you would be lucky if any of them spend a pound a day. They stick on a twenty pence accumulator and stand there all day, mainly to get out from under their wife's feet. Or to keep themselves warm on my electric bill. Fifty guys spending fifty pence a day, doesn't pay for much champagne and cigars Danny boy. Or even extra hours for board-markers' He drove away with a smug grin on his fat red nosed face. I secretly hoped he had gout.

This lack of work was becoming a problem with Patricia and me. I was making a real effort, although it probably didn't seem like that. There was nothing doing with my da, his firm was barely managing to keep him Donnie and Dunky on. After I had finished with them Charlie worked with them for a while but he had been laid off as well. I went to the job centre every single day. There was nothing, zilch, nada. The only way to get a job was if you knew somebody who knew somebody. And most of the people I knew weren't working, well not legitimately anyway. Charlie was forever at me to join him and Searcher on the occasional job, claiming it was easy money. Easy money or not I refused to contemplate a life of crime, I had O' levels.

'So what was down the job centre then, there must have been something' Patricia said the minute I walked in the door.

'Will you at least let me get in and get a cup of tea, before you start moaning at me' I said walking into the kitchen.

'I have got £1.84 in my purse, and it's four days before we get our giro do you want steak and chips for dinner, or should we rough it with lobster thermathingwy' she asked. I wondered if she was learning this sarcastic undertone from me or whether she had always had it.

'Why?' I asked her before I could stop myself. I knew what her reaction was going to be.

'Why, what do you mean why. Are you asking why I've got £1.82 in my purse? Because you aren't bloody working, and I don't mean standing talking to the rest of the wasters in the bookies on a Saturday and handing me £12.00' she ranted.

'£1.84' I said pedantically.

'What about £1.84, how is that an answer?' she further ranted.

'You said £1.84 the first time and then changed it to £1.82, I was only pointing that out' I said with further pedantry.

'Are you joking with me, I tell you I've got' she hesitated and thought for a second 'A handful of coins in my purse that probably isn't enough to pay for our dinner tonight, and your response to that is to correct me about the amount being wrong by two pence. Is that it? Is that the best you can do? Well tell me this oh wise one how is that superior wisdom of yours gonny make' she hesitated again '£1.84 last the rest of the week' she said triumphantly, I suppose the fact that she got the right amount this time was the reason for her being triumphant.

‘I need to get a cup of tea and think about it, okay. Can you let me sit down for gods’ sake’ I said finally making it into the kitchen.

She changed her tack then and made an attempt to be more reasonable I thought. ‘Let me make you a cup, what do you take in it again?’ she asked sweetly.

I sensed a trap but was too dumb to avoid it ‘You know what I take, milk and two sugars. Why are you asking? In fact I know why you’re asking. We haven’t got any milk have we? You’re trying to be wide.” I said with my own sense of triumph.

‘Yes darling, you’re right again, we haven’t got any milk, but you forgot to mention that we have no tea bags and no sugar either. So do you want a glass of warm water?” she asked with sarcasm dripping like venom from her tongue. ‘Well you canny have one, the kettles broke’

How the hell did the kettle get broke if you haven’t got the stuff to make tea’ I asked.

‘It isnae broke, I was being you and trying to be smart’ she said, looking at me with loathing in her eyes.

‘What has happened to her?’ I thought, ‘Probably because she is up the duff’ I answered myself.

‘Go and nip into your ma’s and get a wee loan of some tea bags milk and sugar then, tell her she will get them back on Thursday when our giro comes.’ I suggested ignoring her loathing, as it was patently hormone induced.

‘No’ she said with not a little anger ‘My ma is sarcastic with me as it is whenever she comes down here. ‘Oh is that your best towels?’ She will say or ‘Oh do you not like pictures or that on the wall, they look awfy bare with nothing on them?' Why haven't you got any light shades up, bare bulbs aren't very nice, I don't think.' Patricia said glumly as she sat on the edge of the bed beside me.

'So what, let her be as sarcastic as she wants, it's her only hobby, apart from the bingo. Go on you know you want a cup of tea as much as I do' I said cajoling her into it.

'What will we do about something to eat' she asked glumly.

'Go down to the paki's shop and get a loaf, six eggs and two tins of beans, that will keep us going for a couple of days, we can have toast and beans and then French toast and beans and then toast and egg, see three nights dinners for £1.84. You only need to be able to think and you can sort any problem out' I said with a reasonable degree of smugness. She probably thought I didn't see her sticking two fingers up at me as she left and I made myself comfortable on the bed.

Our bed is in the kitchen, did I tell you that? We have a room and kitchen in McCulloch Street. The living room was massive probably about six by four; the kitchen was a bit smaller but still a half decent size.

We had decided when we first moved in that if we had visitors that it was more practical to have the bed in the kitchen out of sight, as opposed to having it in the living room. We thought about having a sort of living room /kitchen and using the front room as a bedroom. But the front room was much bigger than the kitchen, so we opted to make it our living room. Both rooms had high ceilings so naturally that made them quite cold and hard to heat. There was a distinct lack of furniture in either room for the first six months.

The kitchen had a double bed, a cooker (Darlene's old cooker with only two rings and the oven working) a sink and the cupboard under it. The living room had an old dirty couch with two matching armchairs, again courtesy of Darlene's midnight flit to Coventry. It also had a two bar electric fire in a fire surround that had come from my ma's back court. One of her neighbours must have thrown it out; getting that up to McCulloch Street on the old Silver Cross pram my ma used to use to take her washing to the laundrette was quite an adventure.

The fireplace was about eight feet long so the only way to move it was to place it across the width of the pram rather than the length. This meant that we took up the whole width of the pavement. So rather than do that we decided it was easier to walk on the road with it. Patricia bailed out early and ducked into her Sisters house in Lambhill Street. That left me pushing the pram with my two youngest brothers Paul and David. Paul was in a good mood all the way up the road because *Shakin Stevens* had recently released *green door* and he loved it and sang it (and danced it) constantly. David was in a bad mood because he was a miserable wee shite who was always in a bad mood and didn't want to help me in the first place, if it wasn't about him then it didn't matter.

He was twelve years old now and an utterly spoiled brat. He was the youngest in the family and got whatever he wanted whenever he wanted it. Paul was only four years older but didn't get half as much as David did. Although he still did okay in comparison to Charlie and I. They didn't need to watch cars when the football was on, or collect empty ginger bottles. They were handed everything on a plate.

It was incredible to me how things had changed since I was twelve. I was lucky to get anything but he got an Atari games console. With which he was an utter twat, he lorded it over his nephews wee Tony and Mark who were virtually the same age as him. And he even tried to tell Charlie and me that we couldn't play with it without his permission. He changed his mind readily, when we grabbed him by a leg each and dangled him out of my ma's living room window. At first he was all bravado insisting that we wouldn't drop him. He had another think when Charlie asked me what the name of the cat was that used to regularly fall out of this window and walk away unscathed.

I told Charlie that its name had been cheeky, which we had since replaced with a new cat called cheeky, but it wasn't fair to compare David to a cat because cats knew how to land properly. Charlie conceded the point but reasonably reminded me that David was more liable to bounce than a cat was. It was at that point he started screaming for my ma and told us we could play with his Atari whenever we wanted. I am sure that's what he said but it was difficult to hear him through his screams, along with his tears and snotters.

Although to be fair if you ask Donnie or Dot they will tell you that Charlie and me were spoiled brats. Because they had to get up early and go and do a job before they went to school and hand the money over to my ma.

Donnie claimed this was a constant situation due to the fact that my da was forever losing his wages down the snooker hall, or drinking them in some shebeen in Dennistoun. So my ma sometimes depended on the money from Donnie's paper round. Dorothy claimed it was more like a whorehouse than a shebeen. And fairly regularly she would be stood outside the close where the shebeen was watching my ma scream blue murder at my da. Screaming, mostly for him to hand over some money, until he had heard enough from my ma and slapped her one. That didn't usually stop her according to Dorothy. Depending how desperate my ma was, they would go at it hammer and tongs. Even when he hit her the way he would hit a man, she simply bounced back up and kept at him. Until my da realised through his drunkenness that the only way to get my ma to go away was to give her some money, otherwise she would go at it forever.

Dorothy also reckoned that they moved something like seven times when she was between 10 and 12 years old. They were almost always evicted for not paying rent. This was despite the fact that my da constantly worked, which was more than most in those days. He worked hard and lived harder. I can't remember any of this; most of it was before I was born. I did see my da raise his hands occasionally, but more often than not, he took his temper out on the furniture or the walls.

I have seen him kick a coffee table to pieces, and I mean pieces, basically firewood was all that was left when he had finished. Most of the bedroom doors and the front door had had more than one panel replaced when he either punched his fist right through them or put his working boot through them with an almighty swing of his boot. There were round gravy stains on the living room walls as a result of him throwing full plates of food at my ma. Usually because she 'looked at him funny' when he came in steaming on a Thursday night, with half of his wages spent. I did see some of that but I wasn't there in the sixties when he was at his drunkest and meanest, thank god.

All the way up shields road David moaned and groaned and complained about the fireplace being too heavy at his end. All he was being asked to do was hold it steady, the pram was taking the weight. I was pushing the pram and he and Paul were walking along on either side of the fireplace holding it steady. It was a nice fireplace, it was made of wood with a nice carved mantelpiece and shelves down either side, the electric fire would sit in the middle between the shelves. I thought Patricia would like it and be really happy when I surprised her with it.

'Why have you brought that piece of junk away up from the midden in your ma's back court to throw it in the midden in our back court she asked me after seeing me David and Paul struggle to bring it in to our living room through the window. As it had proved to be too long to manoeuvre through the narrow entrance at the front door.

"What do you mean' I asked breathlessly 'You said you wanted a fireplace for on the living room wall opposite the couch'

'I said I wanted a nice white oak fireplace with smoked glass shelves and a matching electric fire, like the one we saw on the telly. No' a refugee from bonfire night. Take that out before the woodworm in it eat the floorboards' she said with disgust, and to add insult to injury she added 'you're worse than my Granda for picking up shite'

It was on the tip of my tongue to ask her, what that said for her since I had picked her up once, but thought better of it. I was sober. Paul stood looking glumly on he knew that if Patricia had her way, that all the effort he had put in getting the bloody thing in through the window would have to be repeated to get it back out. I might have had some sympathy with him if he wasn't also standing slurping a big ball of spit in and out of his mouth, which was his newest trick. I wonder why he didn't have a girlfriend yet.

David stood there smirking. He hadn't put in any effort so he wasn't bothered. He was clearly waiting for his chance to tell Patricia that he had told me, the fireplace was shite and that Patricia would probably go mental if I took it home without letting her see it first. He might have only been twelve but he was self-righteous wee arse already, and he would only get worse.

'Don't stand their smirking you self-righteous wee arse' I said to him 'I will make you smirk on the other side of your face in a minute' I don't know what that meant but my da was forever saying it to me.

'Can you paint it' Patricia asked.

'Paint what, his smirk' Paul asked her. Patricia gave him her *stare,* her *do you seriously want to piss me off* stare. It was my turn to smirk, that stare was normally for me alone. Paul almost went white that would teach him a valuable lesson.

David laughed out loud at Paul's misfortune. Paul kicked him on his right thigh, he aimed for his balls but David was quick, I will give him that. Within seconds they were rolling about the floor, kicking biting and gouging at each other. I was smiling now it was bringing back happy memories of me and Charlie. Anyway Paul was winning so I thought I would let it go for a few minutes and let David be taught a lesson. Patricia thought differently she lifted Paul up bodily off the floor by the scruff of his neck and pushed him down on one of the armchairs. She then told David to sit on the other armchair. Well that's what she meant when she said 'And you sit over there you annoying wee shite'

'Did you not notice them knocking lumps out of each other right in front of you' she asked me, out of breath with her exertions.

'Who?' I asked with a grin.

This got her angry, me being facetious or sarcastic like that always makes her angry, it's the main reason I do it and enjoy it so much. She is a ridiculously easy person to get angry, and I never tire of it. Ever.

'Can it be painted' she asked again.

I answered that of course it could it was made of wood so as long as it was sanded down properly and we used gloss paint it would look lovely when it was painted.

'Good' she said 'Throw it back out of the window and maybe some idiot will take it and paint it' She almost got me, I was about to get angry but then I spotted her sly smile and realised she was playing me at my own game.

'If you paint it black and it looks okay, we will keep it, but if looks crap painted then out it goes' she said by way of compromise.

'Maybe you should try the same with Danny, paint him black and if he disnae suit it pap him out as well, and since he's already manky it widnae take that much paint' David said, demonstrating his wonderful sense of humour. Idiot that he was. I ignored him, a tactic I should have employed more often.

'Okay' I said 'I will get some black paint from somewhere and do it up. In the meantime, Paul help me to push it against the wall where it will be sitting so we can see how it looks'

Patricia studied it when it was in place and said 'Maybe it doesn't look that bad against the wall and I suppose it goes with the suite in a sort of, we-belong-in-the-same-tip sort of way. I smiled to myself, it wasn't always obvious to her yet, but she would learn that I knew what she liked better than she did. As well as knowing what she wanted or needed, again before she did.

Of course as soon as the fireplace was accepted as being worthy of remaining in our palace Patricia set about getting ornaments to clutter it up. She got some crystal ornaments from her ma, which her ma claimed were family heirlooms. Patricia's aunt Sarah told us that, the ornaments were given as mini bingo prizes down at the cap bingo a few years before Patricia had started working there. I know who I believed. The same Aunt Sarah bought Patricia some lovely wee white sort of porcelain ornaments in the shape of ladies with parasols. They didn't look cheap either. And they probably weren't Sarah was always pleading poverty but she was more careful with money than an Aberdonian with short arms and deep pockets.

So along with a few other trinkets that her granny and other aunties gave her, and I think my ma even gave her something out of the display cabinet in her house. She was able to make the fireplace and indeed the living room look a wee bit more presentable. So it made what happened on a Friday night a couple of weeks later a bit of a tragedy really.

I still couldn't find any work and I was genuinely trying my heart out. I still managed to go out and play darts on a Tuesday night, but only because I would be sitting moping about all day Tuesday until one or other of my brothers would turn up and insist that he would stand me a few pints. I invariably went out with no money at all on a Tuesday and came in pissed with a fish supper for Patricia and a couple of quid in my pocket. The fish supper would be cold as I had carried it all the way from the Yellow bird chippy at the Toll up to McCulloch Street. But it was no problem heating it up in the oven when it worked.

The weekends however were different Donnie and Dunky most often went out together. Mostly to a choice of three or four pubs on the Paisley road, Dunky was constantly on the pull, even though he was winching another bird from Govan, Helen her name was. She was similar to his first wife, skinny and pretty, but not as psychotic. Charlie went out with iris on a Friday night. When I had been working or I managed to get a wee turn here and there Patricia and I would join them most Fridays. The lassies weren't too happy at the fact that we almost always started in *'The Quaich bar'* where me and Charlie would play darts for a couple of hours. But they brightened up when we went to some of the pubs that had a bit of music, like *'Burns' cottage'* or occasionally *'The grand old Opry'* which was always a laugh.

They had gun fights and everything, and there were always a few people dressed up as Indians as well. I do regret that I wasn't there the night that a guy dressed up as Colonel Custer had a right ding dong on the dance floor with a guy dressed up as Geronimo; apparently Colonel Custer had had an unappreciated squeeze at Geronimo's squaws arse. Geronimo then took umbrage at that and started chasing Custer around the hall with a plastic tomahawk, apparently Custer didn't realise it was plastic. Some of the other cowboys, trying to be helpful, set up a circle of chairs in the middle of the dance floor and Custer went inside the circle as Geronimo ran round the outside trying to lamp him one with his tomahawk. Charlie and Iris had been there that night; he told me all about it. Ordinarily I wouldn't have believed a word he said, but Iris swore it was all true. And Charlie was laughing so hard that I believed him.

But now that I wasn't working I would sit in the house in a bad mood most Friday nights. The only time I wouldn't be in a mood was the odd time when Donnie, Dunky and Charlie would show up after the pubs closed to play cards. Most Friday nights followed a distinct pattern; I would be in a restless bad mood until the pubs shut. I would mump and moan at Patricia all night that the telly was rubbish on a Friday, that was providing that we had fifty pence to put in the telly more often than not we didn't. Then I would pace up and down at the window in the living room like an over-excited puppy, hoping that my brothers would turn up with a few cans of lager and a deck of cards.

Like with most things, in fact, like with *ALL* things, my brothers and I were fiercely competitive when playing cards. We only really played two games, *Chase the lady* and *fat*. Anybody who plays cards will know that *Chase the lady* is another name for *Hearts*; this was a game which was played as individual players. *Fat* however was played in pairs, rather like bridge but without the bidding. It was a game that as far as I could tell only Scaffolders played. In fact I can't ever remember playing it with anybody else other than Scaffolders called McCallister. My da played it as did both of his brothers; all of the boys and one of the girls in my family played it.

Like most card games it has an element of skill and an element of luck. When you win it's because you are skilful at the game and when you lose it's because you were unlucky. At least that's the way that McCallister's look at it. The big problem being that some of us were bad losers, in fact all of us were very bad losers. But Donnie and Charlie were also bad winners. They couldn't just win and pocket the cash. They had to continually analyse how they had played some brilliant tactics to win and how whoever they had beat had played some rubbish tactics to lose and were barely worthy of playing in the same room as them.

This didn't cause problems all of the time due to the fact that Dunky and I didn't normally take it as serious as them. Well not to the extent that we would argue about it. We were normally laid back about it, win or lose. However when we were on the same team this particular Friday night against Donnie and Charlie, and they won six games in a row, and became insufferable eejits, we weren't as laid back as usual.

I mean they were being really insufferable eejits, for example Donnie pinched my cheeks and handed me ten pence and said 'Here son, go and get a wee sweetie and when you grow up I will teach you how to play fat' Then to rub salt in the wound Charlie danced around the coffee table whooping like a Red Indian and saying 'heap big trouble for professor Danny, his heap big brains have all dried up'

Dunky said 'Sit down Charlie and stop being a tube, you'se got a bit lucky big deal. Start a new game, your luck canny last all night'

Charlie being the bad winner he is said 'I will sit down when I finish my wee rain dance'

Dunky again said 'For Christ's sake Charlie sit down on your arse'

Charlie took his usual belligerent stance and said 'Who is gonnae making me, you?' And typically I rose to the challenge and said 'Me' and head butted him. Mayhem ensued.

Charlie hit me back with a big left hook that I wasn't expecting. I had expected him to go down when I head butted him, most people did. But Charlie knew me well enough to be on the move backwards a split second before I connected. Dunky stepped in trying to stop us fighting. I don't know if Donnie realised that or if he thought that Dunky was going for Charlie. Either way he lamped Dunky with a lovely right hook of his own, which was a bit sneaky really.

Dunky hadn't even been arguing never mind fighting. So now all four of were into it, which was highly abnormal. Usually two of us would be fighting while the other two tried to break them apart. Also, nine times out of ten it would be either me or Charlie fighting Donnie or Dunky. Charlie and I usually took each other's sides as did they. So this was a completely off kilter fight, with all four of us scrapping and me fighting Charlie and Donnie fighting Dunky. The only thing that could and did make it stranger was Patricia getting out of her bed and screaming at us 'I'm pregnant and that's my new ornaments'

We stopped and looked at the floor; most of her ornaments were in pieces on the floor. The smoked glass centre of the coffee table had a huge crack in it, which gave way as silence fell and both halves fell to the floor. Charlie grinned and said 'oops' Patricia went crazy she got in amongst them and started slapping all three of them and screaming at them to get out of her house and that they were never getting back in again. She shouted at them that she had practically nothing, but what little she did have they smashed up for a bit of a laugh. She told them she hated them and she never wanted to see them again.

A bit over the top if you asked me, it was only a few ornaments. She hadn't asked me. The three of them picked up their jackets and left sheepishly, apologising profusely as they went. I followed them into the close merely to tell Charlie what an arse he had been and how it was entirely his fault. Patricia's sobs brought me back in. I gave her a cuddle and told her I would get them to replace everything. I also told her that they were genuinely sorry; this became slightly unbelievable when we could hear all three of them singing *'Wild Rover'* at the top of their voices as they made their way out of our street.

My smile didn't work nor did my promises to replace everything that got broken with new and better things. She raged and she wept for at least half an hour. I thought she was making too big a deal of it. Of course I did, I was nineteen. What was the major crisis about a few tacky ornaments getting knocked over? I suppose what I didn't, or couldn't understand at the time was that she had been psychologically building a nest. I have since learned that women do that when they are pregnant. And along came me and my brothers and sort of shit in her nest. No wonder she was raging at me and them.

Charlie was at our front door first thing the next morning, with a box of Quality Street and thirty quid. He came in singing *'It's my party, and I'll cry if I want to'* and was instantly forgiven as he always was. He gave Patricia a wee hug, a kiss on the cheek and said 'Sorry about the mess we made hen, I hope that nothing got broke that canny be replaced' She smiled at him and told him 'It was mostly cheap stuff and not to worry, sometimes things canny be helped' and she also told him that he didn't have to rush over here this early, it wasn't as if it was a big deal or anything.

How does he do it? The fight was definitely his fault; anything that got broke was also definitely his fault. So how come Patricia was telling him it was okay and almost apologising to him because he had to come over. He merely grinned his grin and said 'Oh by the way, I bought a car' and walked to the window and held back the curtains to show us. It was a red *Ford Escort*, not a brand new car, probably ten years old or maybe older but it looked brilliant to me. 'Come on I will take you for a spin' he said. Patricia said no she was going to her ma's to do a washing, as we still didn't have a machine.

'Have you not got a washing machine yet' he asked 'I bought Iris a new Hotpoint front loader the other day, she loves it'

'Where are you getting all the money, as if I need to ask' I said, determined that Patricia should realise that the new car and the washing machine were probably the result of some thievery or other. He touched the side of his nose with his finger and said 'Ask no questions, hear no lies' and laughed. 'You know where I got the money anyway, I did a wee turn with Searcher and big Bobby, I asked you if you wanted to come with me, But Saint Danny said no, so don't greet about it now' he said treating me as if it was me that was the idiot, we would see who was the idiot when he got the jail one of these times.

I declined on his offer of a run out in the car as well, he had annoyed me now. After he had gone Patricia asked me 'What do you think him and searcher did' I looked at her full of hurt.

'Does it matter' I asked 'What would be okay for him to have done, in your eyes I mean. What price is alright to pay for a washing machine? Breaking into a factory? Breaking into somebody's house? Stealing a load of gear from a van? Or what about mugging an old woman for her pension?'

Now she looked at me with hurt 'He doesn't mug old woman, that's a nasty thing to say'

It had been a nasty thing to say because a few weeks previously her granny had been mugged on Govan Road when she was coming home from the bingo. Her granny had made the mistake of trying to hold on to her bag and the arsehole who mugged her knocked her to the ground and dragged her along as she tried in vain to keep a grip on the bag. There was nothing of any value in it, less than a pound in cash in fact. But there was a wee school photo of her latest great grandchild which she wanted to keep. She didn't get to keep the bag what she got to keep was a broken arm and bruises all over her face.

'How do you know, he doesn't mug old women?' I asked, in no mood to let Charlie get away with demeaning me because I wouldn't get involved with him and Searcher.

Patricia realised that I was angry and probably why I was angry. 'You know he doesn't' she said softly 'But you're right we will get a washing machine and a tumble drier as well one of these days without stealing to do it'

'Aye' I replied 'And a car'

Patricia smiled and said 'We canny run to a car right now, but at least we can get teabags and milk' and held up the money Charlie had given her, slightly missing the point.

Dunky also turned up later that afternoon also with a box of chocolates and twenty quid for Patricia to replace the ornaments. And again he charmed her into the situation where she was apologising to him for making such a fuss about nothing. An hour after he had left I was stood at the window and spotted Donnie coming along the street.

'If he gives you chocolates and more money, maybe we will be able to afford a car' I said.

What was I thinking, it was Donnie. He gave her a kiss on the cheek and a co-op bag full of ornaments, which we later discovered had come from his own house. Annie was livid with him, apparently he had got up that morning and told her that he had broken all of Patricia's ornaments and that he was giving her the ones that they had. And calmly put them all into a carrier bag and left with them.

Luckily for us the only ornaments that didn't get broke were the ones that Patricia's aunt Sarah had given her, which coincidentally were the only ones Patricia liked or cared about. So thanks to Charlie and Dunky were fifty quid better off and all we had to replace was the coffee table. Which we did, we bought one with ceramic tiles on the top from a shop in the town for twelve quid.

The thirty eight quid left over allowed us to live like royalty for a week. We even bought a half pound of butter instead of a tub of Blue Band margarine. It was a pity that after four days we could no longer afford bread to spread the butter on.

'Danny, you need to take the money away from me and you decide what we need every day.' Patricia said as I opened the envelope that contained my latest giro. It was for £56, which had to last us two weeks. Patricia was now four months pregnant and had cut down her shifts at the bingo. Her job there was as a floor runner. For any of you unaware of bingo halls, when somebody shouts house and holds there card up in the air. A floor runner literally runs over to where they are and shouts out all the numbers on the card so that the caller can check them and declare it a legitimate claim.

The floor runner then runs down to the bottom of the hall and collects a prize slip detailing the amount won by the successful punter. They then run back to wherever the punter is sitting and give them the prize slip, the winner then claims their prize from the cashiers at the end of the night. By the time the prize slip is collected and delivered the game has moved on and it is very likely that someone else has called house and the runner starts all over again. As you can imagine, this isn't an ideal job for a pregnant teenager.

Perhaps if there had been a better or kinder manager in the capitol bingo hall in Lorne Street then a different job could have been found for Patricia. Perhaps behind the tea bar or sitting down selling tickets anything but a floor runner. It was more the assistant manager that was at fault. It was her that decided what tasks everyone was suited to but unfortunately one night a few months previously, at the Christmas night out. She had overheard me calling her a dried up old spinster. I was only joking she was in her thirties and she hadn't had a boyfriend for almost a year. She didn't find me funny and had taken that stupid remark out on Patricia ever since.

So my giro was for £56 a fortnight, Patricia earned about £30 a week. Our rent was £24 a week, electric and gas amounted to about £8 a week. The telly was a coin operated one which took fifty pence pieces, probably about one a day if we watched it a lot. That was another £3 a week. Out of the £58 a week we had coming in we had about £23 a week to feed us and clothe us, and pay for all the household things like soap and toilet paper and bleach and all that.

I improvised, it didn't bother me to use washing up liquid as a temporary shampoo when needed, it did bother Patricia but. She had beautiful straight blonde hair which reached half way down her back, which she was very particular about and spent hours looking after. So she did object when I suggested that there wasn't any difference between lemon Squeezy and Vo5 or Sunsilk or finesse shampoos, it was probably all made in the same factory and they only changed the labels not what was in the bottles. She pointed out that even if I was right, we couldn't even afford lemon Squeezy it was far too dear.

The result was that we basically had less than twenty quid a week to live on. New clothes were a complete fantasy. Patricia at one point had to fill her shoes with a sheet of cardboard because there was a hole in the bottom. What was particularly strange about that was that we experimented with various things like a piece of lino or a piece of corrugated cardboard from a heavy carton. We eventually decided that two sheets of thin cardboard like a Cornflakes box was best, because it was thick enough to stop stones cutting your feet but thin enough so that your shoe still fitted you. It only took us a few weeks to become experts in cardboard and we thought nothing of it.

The situation became even more dire when Patricia was five months pregnant and I insisted that she packed her job in. I insisted for two reasons, the first being that she had started fainting all over the place. One minute she would be stood beside me the next she was crumpled on the floor. Her doctor, who was a quack at the best of times, told her it was a symptom of pregnancy and that was that. It wasn't a symptom of pregnancy in any of the books I could find in the library. But she wouldn't let me go in and tell the old fool.

The second reason was much more ominous and haunts me to this day. It was a Monday night, I wasn't doing anything in particular but as usual we were skint. Patricia was working until ten and I offered to meet her and we could walk home together. She decided that she was a bit tired, she was five months pregnant after all, and that she would rather get the bus home. So there was no point me meeting her because that meant both of us having to pay bus fare, so it was decided that she would get the bus home alone.

She finished slightly later because the dried up old spinster was being a madam about something or other. By the time she got to the bus stop it was ten thirty, the last bus to Pollokshields was supposed to be ten twenty but lucky for her the bus arrived at the stop at the same time as she did. The bus was empty, apart from her and the driver, she thought nothing of it, sometimes the last bus was quiet and it was a miserable wet night for anybody to be out.

She did notice the driver adjust his mirror so that he appeared to be looking at her rather than traffic, which did make her feel slightly uncomfortable. She started to panic when the driver turned off the Paisley Road west on to Seaward Street but then instead of going straight along Seaward Street and up Shields road he took a sharp right turn into Milnpark Street.

Milnpark Street was a long dark side street full of warehouse and factories, the bus was not routed to go down it, Patricia got very scared. She walked down to where the drivers cab was and said 'you could have told me the bus was terminating here I was going all the way to the top of Shields Road'.

The driver stayed silent for a few seconds, frightening her even more, she looked around for a button that would open the door, she knew there was one, but she couldn't see it.

'I could take you up Shields Road darling, if you like' the driver said with a hitch in his breath.

'No let me off here, my man is walking down Shields road to meet me he will probably keep walking and come down here thinking I've missed the last bus' she knew that didn't make sense she had only just told him she was going to the top of Shields Road, but she was beginning to panic.

'Oh he won't be looking for this bus hen, the Pollokshields bus was twenty minutes ago, I had this one out on a wee trial run after it got a new engine, it sounds lovely and smooth doesn't it. She had no idea what to say or what to do, she still couldn't find an exit button or lever or anything.

'Aye I suppose it does sound smooth mister, but can you let me off here then and I can maybe catch up with my man, please' she said trying not to sound scared , which was almost impossible.

'Aye hen no bother I will let you off here but do you know think we should have a wee bit of a kiss and a cuddle first, you're a right wee cracker so you are.' Patricia then did panic and lunged towards the door which miraculously whooshed open. She doesn't know whether she triggered them to open by pushing on them or whether the driver accidentally opened them as he tried to leave his seat.

She ran, behind her she heard the engine of the bus rev up but it became silent as she reached the corner of Seaward Street and Milnpark Street and almost bumped into an elderly couple walking slowly along towards Shields road. She hesitated about telling them of her ordeal because what could they really do about it. The old man or even the old woman might try and go and shout at the driver or something but what would be the point of that. She started chatting to the old couple about how miserable a night it was and decided to walk all the way up Shields road with them.

A bus did pass them about halfway up the road but it was past them before Patricia could see who was driving, not that she wanted to look anyway. The old man remarked that the bus was running very late. When she eventually got home, I was lying asleep on the couch, with the telly blaring away. She started shouting at me that she was out working her fingers to the bone and all I could do was lie and sleep and waste all our money by having the telly on and not even watch it.

I was stunned, she was never like this. I presumed it was the dried up old spinster who had upset her again and kept her late it was nearly half past eleven. I gave her a wee cuddle and made her a cup of tea and that's when she broke down and told me what had happened. She was adamant that she hadn't encouraged the drivers attention, I felt bad that she even thought she had to defend herself and tell me that.

I was as angry as I had ever been in my life. The nearest bus garage was on Polmadie road very near the masonic hall we had our wedding reception in. I was all for running down there and seeing if anybody was still there. But what would have been the point only Patricia could recognise the driver and she was in no state to go with me. I wanted to go along to the phone box and call the police. She said no, she wanted to have a bath go to bed and forget about it. I eventually calmed down and let it go, for now.

The next morning I made her some tea and toast and then insisted that she come along to the bus garage with me so we could find out if there was any way to identify the driver. After I did a bit of shouting and bawling we eventually got to speak to a manager. He told us that there were three hundred drivers worked out of this garage alone and this was only one of six in the city. He took our details but stated that there was very little chance of him finding anything out. Patricia couldn't give a very good description of him because she only seen him side on sitting down. She didn't even know if there was a number or destination on the front of the bus. We admitted defeat and left his office.

After half an hour of standing at the gateway into the garage and me asking 'is that him' Patricia got fed up and insisted that we go home. Since that day I have been arrested four times by the police. Three out of those four times were for assaulting bus drivers. Not because I thought any of them was the guy who frightened Patricia, but because I don't like bus drivers anymore. Thankfully I don't use public transport very much nowadays.

The end result of all this trauma was that I wouldn't let her go back to work. She insisted that she should and to my surprise, when the dried up old spinster heard what had happened she said that Patricia should come back and she would put her on ticket sales so that she could leave early and I could see her get home alright. I said it didn't matter she wasn't working anymore and that was that.

As she was entitled to one week's pay in lieu of notice and one week's holiday money, it was three weeks before she could sign on and get any dole money. So we had to miss two weeks rent and were starting to worry about losing our house. Patricia still had a tendency to faint on a regular basis. This was the root cause of me almost being arrested at the social security office.

We were skint and desperate and to make matters worse the bru was on strike. Well strictly speaking not all of the bru only the part that sent out the giros. It was apparently part of a civil servants strike probably something to do with the bitch of hell, Maggie Thatcher that is, not the other bitch from hell that was sitting in front of me refusing me a counter payment.

'I have been to Martha street missus, they told me I was entitled to a counter payment due to *'extraordinary hardship'* 'I quoted from the slip of paper I had indeed been given at Martha Street. Where incidentally and ironically I had been sent by the very eejit sitting in front of me who now told me that I had to go back there.

'I know what they told you at Martha Street, but they were wrong. If they did want to authorise an emergency hardship payment, they would have given you a CF1670 form to give to me' she said with the smugness of a very very smug person.

'You are fucking making up forms now you bastard, I bet CF1690 doesn't even exist' I shouted at her standing up and banging the Plexiglas between her and me.

'It's a CF1670 not 1690, the 1690 only gets you a glass of orange' the guy next to me said with a huge grin.

'What?' I said to him bewildered.

'1690, Orange? Do you no' get it he said.

'Do I look as if I am in the mood for stupid jokes you stupid bastard' I said to him. 'My wife is six months pregnant, she has fainted four times today, she has twenty two pence in her purse, this stupid bastard here' I indicated the woman behind the Plexiglas 'she thinks I am going to walk all the way over to Martha Street for another form while I watch my wife faint another three times. And you think you that's a good time to make a joke about king fucking Billy, do you?' I was now flat out apoplectic.

'No offence wee man, know what I mean. A jokes a joke pal' he says holding his hand out palms up. He wasn't the real reason for my anger anyway so I turned away from him and towards the real reason for my anger, the bitch from hell (not Thatcher).

'Give me my fucking giro you pathetic waste of space you reject bitch from secretarial college, give me my giro' I screamed at her punching the Plexiglas in front of me again. She stood up and backed away.

The king Billy joker beside me who had no sense whatsoever of when to stay out of things said 'That's unbreakable, there's no point in punching it'

'Is that fucking right, unbreakable you say' I said and proceeded to pick up the plastic chair with metal legs that I happened to have been sitting on and used it to set about the window with wild abandon.

After about five minutes of swinging the chair as hard as I could, and then throwing the chair from ever increasing distances as hard as i could. Then standing on the chair and trying to kick the window into submission, running at the window and trying flying karate kicks. I finally conceded his point that the window was indeed unbreakable. The police arrived with perfect timing to see me land on my arse following my last karate kick as they restrained me by grabbing one arm each and proceeded to drag me away I spat on the window and said 'I am not finished with you, you see through transparent bastard, I will be back' The rest of the people who were also mostly waiting for their own giro's gave me a spontaneous round of applause. Patricia, I noticed, didn't join them.

'Did you think that would get you a giro any quicker son' the first policeman asked me, sympathetically shaking his head. They had taken me into a private interview room and radioed in for a van to come and take me to the nearest nick.

'I wasn't getting a giro anyway' I said 'That stupid bitch that was serving me was sitting there enjoying me begging too much. I have been here since nine o'clock this morning. My wife is six months pregnant she has fainted six times today already. I said *(I know I said four times earlier, in fact it was only twice but it doesn't do any harm to exaggerate sometimes*)

'I think the reason she is fainting might be hunger, and what is that doing to my wean that's inside her. Ask yourself that.' I added. (*We had enjoyed a burger and chips earlier from the roll van near the United cash and carry, but I was trying to make a point, which telling the truth wouldn't really help*)

'Would you no' be angry big man' I asked the second policeman, who shrugged his shoulders and raised his eyebrows. *(Getting any help or sympathy from him was going to be a long shot)*

'But would you no', after all it's been 18 days since my last giro which was for £56. My wife has got 22p in her purse and we are four weeks behind with the rent. If it was nearer Christmas I would be looking for a stable with a manger in it' I said smiling but had no takers. (*A hard audience these two*)

'The point is guys the bitch behind the counter sent me over to Martha Street three times today *(twice really)* and I had to watch my wife fainting about eight times, what do you expect me to do, buy her flowers, the bitch I mean not my wife.' I knew I was flogging a dead horse and started to worry about how Patricia was going to manage to get home on her own when they lifted me. I wondered if they would let me phone Charlie to come and get her. Bastards probably wouldn't because they were bastards.

Some suit popped his head around the corner and gestured to policeman number one. He went out into the corridor while policeman number two decided to stare at me. I have no clue why that seemed like a good idea to him, it wouldn't have been my idea of fun but each to their own, I suppose. The suit was muttering to policeman number one, but not quietly enough not to be heard.

'There's been an error' he said with hesitation.

'What kind of error' policeman number one asked.

'The young man in there was indeed entitled to a counter payment and it said so, on the paperwork that he had brought back from Martha Street. Aileen, that's the girl that was dealing with him, failed to notice' the suit said, at least sounding apologetic.

'So what?' policeman number one asked and said 'that doesn't give him the right to be an arse and try to wreck the joint'

'No it doesn't, but his wife is six months pregnant and she has fainted several times today' the suit said.

'Ten times' I shouted.

Policeman number two decided staring wasn't enough and punched me on the side of the thigh, giving me a dead leg, the rotten bastard. I used to hate that at school when some eejit sneaked up on you and kneed you on the thigh, giving you a dead leg. And funnily enough I still hated it even though I was now in my twenties.

'You gave me a dead leg you rotten bastard' I said to policeman number two.

'I know' he said and laughed 'I used to hate that when people did it to me at school'

'Snap, you bastard' I said trying to resuscitate my leg by rubbing it.

The suit and policeman number one came back into the room. The suit said 'I think under the circumstances, considering that nothing was broken despite all the effort he put in to trying to break whatever he could, that we won't press charges in this instance' this didn't please either of the policemen.

'It's not up to you sir, when we entered the waiting room, master McCallister here was mid- flight with a kung-Fu style flying kick at the window. Which was admittedly unsuccessful and he landed on his skinny arse. Therefore we both, indicating him and his sadistic dead legging pal, witnessed him attempting malicious damage to the window' policeman number one said very righteously.

'Yes but as I am in charge of the window, I don't wish to press charges, so let's call it a day constable' the suit said trying to use whatever authority he presumed that he had. But he was dealing with a power hungry Glasgow policeman. The suit had no authority but was middle class enough to think that he had.

'Technically sir, it is not your window it is a window paid for by the taxpayer. So it isn't your choice it is the choice of the taxpayer' policeman number two said, obviously keen to let us all know that it wasn't only his pal who was a dickhead.

‘Can I maybe mention that my da and two brothers worked up in Sullom Voe last year? And the amount of tax they paid was absolutely scandalous. So since they are significant taxpayers, I would like to point out that none of them would press charges either’ I said with triumph. If the guy in charge of the window didn't want to press charges and the taxpayers represented by my da didn't want to, then who else was there that would.

Policeman number two was not happy at my point and stood up, probably to tell me he was unhappy. Now I normally give people the benefit of the doubt when accidents happen, but I don’t entirely think it was an accident, that he stood on my foot as he got up. I had cheap trainers on and he had size eleven tackety boots. His feet won the one sided and uneven contest; he broke two of my toes. Not that I knew he had broken my toes but I knew that it was damned sore. So when I did appear in front of the custody sergeant it was on a charge of police assault and resisting arrest, not criminal damage to the window I didn’t damage.

Even my lawyer agreed with me that it was a stretch to charge me with police assault when I had two broken toes. Policeman number two, who obviously got bullied at school (the prick) claimed that I had kicked him on the sole of his boot and that’s how I ended up with two broken toes, and since the imprint of the sole of his boot was indeed imbedded on the toe of my trainer. There was evidence to substantiate his claim. When I pointed out to the desk sergeant that the imprint of the boot could just as easily have come from policeman number two stamping on my foot. The sergeant explained that to believe an ignorant lying scumbag like me would mean that he would have to disbelieve an honest hard working pillar of the community like policeman number two.

Which I conceded was a fair point and entirely understandable. I shook hands with policeman number two and said I hoped to meet him again sometime, but hopefully when he wasn't in uniform and didn't have any of his ugly homosexual pals with him. He then dragged me down to the cells where I again assaulted him. This time I used my face and ribs to severely bruise the knuckles of his right hand. I also got to pay a £120 fine at two pounds a week for the privilege.

Patricia got handed the giro after I had been lifted, and she told me the next day when I got out that the suit had gave her two quid to get a taxi home. She got the bus and kept the two quid. So that was handy that she had kept me the first week's payment for my fine.

Chapter twenty six; when a child is born.

Our struggles didn't decrease as Patricia endured her seventh and eighth months of pregnancy. In fact if anything they got worse. She wasn't working at all now, I still couldn't find a bloody job, and even the so called job in the bookies was still only on a Saturday shift. The money we got from the social security was pathetic. I have no idea how anybody was supposed to live on that. Charlie wanted me to go back to the social and scam them out of some more furniture or get hardship grants or something. But I was sick of begging from them, I wanted to work. I didn't want hand outs, I didn't want to con anybody not even the social. I only wanted a bloody job. It didn't even matter what kind of job, as long as it was a bloody job.

I could see people round about me, some who were older and some younger, settle into a workless pattern of life. I did the same. Up early every morning get a newspaper if I could afford it. I bought the Express because it had a very good crossword page which could sometimes take me half the day to finish. Spend the afternoon in the bookies with a pound trying to turn it into a tenner, by betting on ten pence doubles or trebles. Back to the house at tea time for whatever meagre meal we could afford. It wasn't that rare that we couldn't afford anything.

We learned to improvise and be really careful with money. For example I would get a big bag of flour every giro day. With which I could make pancakes or scones every day which would at least ensure we ate something. Near the end of the fortnight when we ran out of money completely and couldn't even afford eggs. I would attempt to make pancakes without them, I don't recommend it. It was a fairly regular occurrence that Patricia would go and 'borrow' an egg from her ma. The consequence I most hated about being out of work and constantly skint was having to borrow money from anybody.

I would avoid it at all costs.

'No, you go and phone her' I said to Patricia 'She moans at me' I was talking about my ma, she didn't really moan at me when I borrowed money from her, well she did but it wasn't about the money. It was about me not working, she never believed or understood how hard I was trying but so was everybody else in Glasgow. My da had never been out of work even when he was drinking heavily and gambling heavily he always worked so my ma would remind me of my obligations to Patricia and now my unborn child whenever I tried to tap her. That was too high a price for me to pay I would rather go to a loan shark and pay 1000 per cent interest than listen to my ma telling me I was letting her down. Even if she was right.

It was relentless; every time we thought we could see a chink of light someone would draw the curtains. I had a decent win on the horses, decent for me anyway. I put a 50p football coupon on and won £80. We splashed out £20 and filled the fridge and the cupboard with food, fresh food canned food packets of flour and rice, the lot. We even got our favourite treat a block of Lurpak butter. When we got back from the Fine Fayre supermarket and started to make our tea, one of the only two rings on the cooker burnt out as did the oven. We were left with a cooker with a single ring that was working. Shit.

£30 went on a cooker and £25 went on a cot, mattress and blankets. The cooker was second hand but the cot and the mattress were both new. I won £80 which was equivalent to two weeks dole money for both of us, it lasted fourteen hours. Shit, shit. This was the pattern of poverty, as soon as you thought you had your head above water some bastard stood on it. In fact let's tell the truth and shame the devil. I am pleading poverty, but we had a roof above our head. We still put about a fiver of our precious dole money in a telly every fortnight. We both smoked, yes we both smoked. Smoking during pregnancy was no big deal. We had visited Annie in hospital the day after she had Mary Jane.

Annie didn't smoke but we did so she came along to the day room and sat with us, the expectant mothers and the recent mothers, all of whom were smoking. One woman had to be almost physically dragged out of the room so severe were her labour pains, she was fighting to be allowed to finish her fag.

So it's not really fair that I plead poverty, we did smoke but not cigarettes. We both smoked roll ups, we would buy a tin of Golden Virginia tobacco and six packets of Rizla cigarette papers and try and make it last us the long and arduous fortnight between giros. Towards the end of the fortnight we would unpick any unfinished roll ups and put the tobacco back into the tin, mix it up with fresh tobacco and eke out a few more skinny roll ups.

I also had to shoulder the blame for regularly having to pay fines for stupidity. Stupidity isn't really a criminal offence except in my case; I found the most obscure ways to get myself in bother. I got a ten pound fine once for urinating in a public place, it was in the middle of Paisley Road West, I mean in the middle of the road. I was standing there completely drunk having a relaxing and much needed pish, when I looked up a police car was facing me. With two big hairy ugly police officers looking at me, the female one looked amused the other one didn't. I carefully shook any drips away and walked to the back of the police car and let myself in.

At least that got me a decent night's sleep. Patricia was now in her ninth month of pregnancy and that meant that only one of us could fit in the double bed and that one wasn't me. She thrashed about like a fish out of water; talking about a fish she seemed to have more limbs than an octopus as well. I would wake up at four in the morning clinging on to a six inch strip of the bed, she would be tangled up in both sheets and wearing the quilt like a Sari. She would then either kick me or slap me and accuse me of wrapping the quilt round her and throwing the pillows on the floor. How I managed to do this with one foot on the floor was miraculous.

A week to go and for once in her life Patricia decides to be do something before she absolutely has to do it.

'Danny, wake up' she said pushing me, hard.

'It wisnae me' I said and turned over, grabbing the quilt while I had a miniscule chance to get a small corner of it.

'DANNY WAKE UP' she screamed 'I'M HAVING PAINS'

It did register, I heard her loud and clear. But my mind and body shut down. I grabbed the quilt and wrapped it around me including my head. Whatever it was she said was reverberating around the room and around the inside of my head. And then it really registered I really heard her. I was up and out the room door and out the front door within a fraction of a second. I was at the phone box outside *'The Honours Three'* pub in less than ten seconds. Alan Wells was a tortoise in comparison to me. I phoned 999 and got through to the ambulance service. I could barely speak; I was breathless and doubled over with a stitch in my side. One of my pals from the bookies Tommy the bunnet, seen me and asked if Patricia had gone into labour, I wheezed and nodded, bastard fags were to blame.

He conveyed the information to the woman on the other end of the phone and asked 'who's with your missus Danny, her ma?' I shook my head and said 'Nobody but I won't be a minute' and then I phoned Charlie to tell him, well not Charlie but his next door neighbour who was not all that interested until I asked him if he had any money put by for his funeral. Because if he didn't go and get Charlie and tell him Danny needed him right away, Charlie would not be a good neighbour in the morning.

I bolted back to the house, Patricia had managed to get herself up and dressed and was sitting on the edge of the bed.

'You don't look to be in that much pain' I said as I watched her roll a fag. 'And by the way, that's a cigar you are rolling not a fag, do you think we are made of money'

She put the makings back in the tin and said 'You do it, but put some tobacco in it, half the time you make it, it's just about only roll up paper and it burns away in seconds'

I looked at her and said 'I thought you were in pain anyway, you are taking it awful well. I had heard that labour pains were sore as well'

'It might no' have been labour pains' she says sheepishly.

I have a flashback to my big sister Dorothy having wee Tony her first wean and everybody being up to high doh. She got took to hospital but was back in the house within the hour, it had been wind.

I looked at Patricia with suspicion and asked her 'Have you farted'

'What is it with you McCallister's' she said 'you'se are all disgusting. If it's not farts its jobbies or snotters you are talking about' she lifted her head and then asked me with a little embarrassed smile on her coupon 'Why?' Can you still smell it' and then she was lying on her back roaring with laughter.

That's when Charlie walked in and said 'Iris was in a lot more pain than that when she was in labour'

The ambulance arrived five minutes after Charlie and the ambulance guys insisted on taking her to the hospital even though they thought it was a false alarm, which it plainly was. Charlie followed us down in the car which was good because it meant he could keep me company and give us a lift home when they told us she was fine and we could go home.

What this farce did do was frighten me enough that I decided we would go and stay at my ma's house until Patricia had the wean, and if my ma didnae like it she could lump it. I went down the next day and threw Paul out of my old room which was now his room. I suppose being in my ma's with the comfort of having her on hand to deal with whatever might happen, was worth having to put up with posters of *Elvis* and hard snotters on the pillows.

The theory was absolutely sound. It was good being in my ma's. There was food in the fridge, the whole house was warm. Patricia's ma was a bit put out, but that was tough. My ma stayed much nearer the southern general and she was on the phone, and on top of that she was my ma. I dragged a single bed into Paul's room, so that Patricia could have the double bed to herself. I lay on that single bed every night staring at her, waiting for a twinge. I stopped getting undressed after the first few nights, and kept my clothes on, and my trainers. My snide trainers by the way, which Charlie mentioned when he showed me his new Adidas Samba trainers the week before when we were at the hospital with Patricia. I liked my Hitec's; Adidas trainers were a waste of money anyway.

Friday night, Donnie, Dunky and Charlie are going along to the *Rolls Royce* social club at the toll. They have recently joined the snooker team in there and have been allowed an associate membership. Those were like gold dust, the *Rolls Royce* social club had new snooker tables, subsidised drinking and a touch of class when compared to the rest of the clubs around the Toll. Did I want to go with them for a game of doubles? Of course I bloody did. Could I? Of course I bloody couldn't. My ma and da were also going out, to the *Viceroy bar,* my ma offered to stay in, just in case. I told her not to worry, nothing had happened all week what was the chances of something happening in the few hours she would be down the pub.

'Danny go and get me a bag of chips' Patricia said, she had been restless and hungry all night. The bag of chips was the latest demand. I had already been at the shops for a packet of *polo mints,* which I think she only asked for because I had told her that they were my ma's craving when she had been pregnant with wee David. Then I got sent out for two packets of *juicy fruit* chewing gum, and then sent out again for a tin of Pineapple chunks. To be perfectly honest she was getting on my nerves. She had also sent Paul for two bags of pickled onion *monster munch* and three bags of 10p crisps preferably *onion rings* she said.

'It's half past eleven' I said, the chippy will be shutting'

'It stays open to twelve now' she said with a whine in her voice I couldn't ignore. 'And anyway even if it is shut the Chinky's is still open, you can get me bag of chips from there.

I smiled through gritted teeth and dragged myself to the chippy, it was indeed open. I bumped into Searcher and Bobby at the chippy. Bobby invited me to his upcoming wedding in six weeks; I gladly accepted and felt a bit guilty that I was losing touch with them. I hadn't seen them for at least six months and they were by far the best mates I had. Charlie still saw them most days and more particularly nights.

'Here baby I put plenty of salt and vinegar on them, just the way you like them and I got you a pickle' I said as I handed over the chips and lay down beside Patricia on the double bed. I watched with awe as she devoured them, she ate like a starving lioness. Less than five minutes and she was done.

'Okay' she says 'I am ready now'

'Ready for what?' I stupidly ask.

She smiles 'to have your wean Danny, go and phone an Ambulance I have been having contractions for about three hours.

I looked at her and smiled 'Good one' I said ''you nearly had me going there'

'Danny go and phone a bloody ambulance, this is starting to get a bit sore' she said and she was telling the truth. Shit.

We made it to the hospital in plenty of time; by the time we got there her contractions had stopped. She was wheeled into the maternity suite and I was asked by the midwife if I wanted to go in with her.

'Why?' I asked her 'Are you short staffed?'

She giggled and said 'No we aren't short staffed, some men like to be present at the birth'

'What for?' I asked panicking slightly; I think this daft nurse is serious. At first I thought she was joking.

'You can hold her hand or wipe her brow, we will find something for you to do' she said walking away and gesturing for me to follow.

There you go, I knew they were short staffed, 'I bet I end up emptying the bed pans' I said to her.

'If you want' she said 'Whatever floats your boat'

Patricia was on the bed lying on her back panting and sweating. I had the briefest thought that this wasn't unlike the way she was during conception, and I grinned to myself.

'What the hell are you grinning at you idiot, does look bloody funny to you?' she screamed at me.

'Hiyah baby, did you miss me?' I asked her.

'When I throw this bed pan at you I won't miss you I promise you that' she said and then made some ooh aah sounds as if she was in pain or something. I managed to get near her without her either hitting me or throwing anything, so that was promising.

'Do you want me to get you anything baby' I asked her with a soothing voice 'A drink of water or more chips maybe' I added smiling, it was a joke. Why then did she look at me as if I had suggested she might want to run a marathon?

'They gave me a suppository' she said. This was obviously something to do with having a baby. I had no idea what a suppository is.

'That's good then isn't it' I said, positively brimming with good cheer.

'No Danny, that isn't fuckin well' she said. *'What now?'* I thought, *'why has she started swearing at me'* maybe a suppository wasn't a good thing after all.

'So what is a suppository' I asked as pleasantly as I could.

'It's something they stick up your bum, to help you do the toilet' she said deeply embarrassed and looking scared.

I was mortified, I was imagining some sort of tube or funnel or something.

'Why are you looking at me like that?' she asked 'You look more scared than I am. They aren't giving you one, could you try and calm down. And even if they do it's only a wee pill. It loosens your bowels and clears your head'

'How can it clear your head, that's ridiculous, before I caught her smile and her meaning. She was implying my head is full of shite. She had a point I suppose.

'I think it's working now Danny, come on help me off this bed and over to the toilet' Patricia said indicating a door behind me marked toilet, that was handy. I looked at the midwife she nodded her head. I will tell you something about that suppository they gave Patricia, it was very fast acting, we only got half way to the toilet when it started working, and I mean it really started working.

The midwife and the nurse almost bundled me out of the delivery room and said they would come back for me when I was needed. Which I thought would be a few minutes maybe half an hour. Two hours later and I was still in the waiting room but now Dunky was with me. He had heard from Paul that I was here and had come along straight from the pub. It was almost two o'clock in the morning when he arrived.

'So what was it?' he asked me, sitting down in a chair opposite me. In fact he collapsed into a chair across from me the way a sack of potatoes does when you drop it.

'What was what?' I answered.

'What flavour of wean was it, a blue one or a pink one?' he slurred all smiles and contentment at his little joke.

'She hasn't had it yet' I said, not all that happy with him that he had turned up here drunk. But it was a Friday night. Dunky didn't do un-drunk Friday nights.

'Good, so they haven't missed anything then?' he asked cryptically.

'Who hasn't missed what? What are you on about' I asked perplexed.

My perplexity didn't last long. 'Danny, congratulations son, well done' Donny said as he approached me across the waiting room. A bottle of something or other in his hand, knowing him it was more likely to be a bottle of Olde England or Lanliq wine than vintage champagne.

'She might no' have had it yet' Charlie advised him 'You know how slow she is at everything, we could be here all weekend'

Exactly what I needed Donnie, Dunky and Charlie all drunk all in a stupidly happy mood for me and disastrously all here, together.

'You're right Charlie, you're not often wrong but you are right gain' Dunky said.

'I know I am right' Charlie said to Dunky 'What am I right about?'

Dunky looked at me puzzled, so I answered 'You are right that she hasn't had the wean, so why don't you three get a taxi and I will phone you all tomorrow and let you know the score'

'No we are here now, we are in it till the bitter end' Donnie said.

'What bitter fucking end' I asked 'There won't be a fuckin bitter end, Patricia is having my son, how can that be a bitter end you stupid old shit' He was only about twelve years older than me, but it seemed to me that Donnie was middle aged from about the age of twenty two. Certainly his dress sense and musical taste was. He not only wore the same jumpers as Val Doonican but I am sure he had a couple of his albums as well. I am also sure he was the original inspiration for the no dad range of clothes. As in no-dad-don't-make-me wear-that-please-don't-dad.

'We could have a game of fat, has anybody got a pack of cards?' Dunky suggested. I didn't really want Patricia to know this but I thought that this wasn't a bad idea. I don't know if this was entirely normal but no matter where we were or what circumstances we were under, at least one of us would normally be able to produce a pack of cards. My whole family played cards, my parents my brothers, obviously, and even my sisters. For many years the favoured way to spend a Sunday evening in our house in Cessnock Street was a game of cards.

The game would only be interrupted by one of two things, Dallas on the TV or a crisis. Not just any crisis either, life or liberty would need to be at stake at least. We would play very simple games like chase the ace or pontoon to begin with, so that the younger children like David and Paul and the nephews Mark and Tony could join in. But come eight o'clock the children were sent to bed and we played the game 'Newmarket' for hours on end. It had an element where a certain card had to be played for a pot to be won and if it wasn't the prize rolled over until the next game. This could build up to a very tidy sum.

We only played for maybe ten pence but the pot could quickly build to a fiver or a tenner and it was hotly contested. Most times with a high pot my ma would constantly be telling each of us to stop calling the others a cheat. It could get very bitter and acrimonious. Given the recent troubles I had experienced with my brothers playing fat. I thankfully came to my senses before any cards were dealt. I imagined how Patricia would react if I started fighting with my brothers over a game of cards, in the waiting room outside the delivery room, and I didn't like what I imagined.

Thankfully we didn't start fighting over a game of cards; it was over a nurse that we started fighting. The nurse that was busily looking after Patricia as a matter of fact, don't get me wrong she was a nice nurse a very pleasant nurse, not exactly a looker but okay. She was exactly Dunky's type of woman; a female.

She had come into the waiting room to let me know that Patricia's contractions had slowed down, and that she was going for a bit of a sleep. Patricia that is, not the nurse. And that she would come and get me if anything changed. The nurse that is, not Patricia. The nurse was finding it more difficult to get rid of Dunky than to look after Patricia.

'Dunky, will you get away from that nurse, she is meant to be looking after Patricia and you are keeping her back from her work' I said pulling at Dunky's arm. 'Anyway what happened to that lassie Helen from Govan you were supposed to be seeing?'

'Helen of Govan with the face that launched a thousand ships' he said sarcastically 'I am still seeing her, I like mince and totties, I really do' he said. I knew this was going somewhere, so I said nothing in reply. I also like pie and chips or egg and chips, but I have them all week. So at the weekend I sometimes have a curry, variety is the spice of life'

'Should that not be curry powder then because that's the spice of life really?' Charlie asked, missing Dunky's point.

'No Charlie what he means is that Helen from Govan is egg and chips and that wee nurse is a chicken Vindaloo' I said smugly.

I never smelled anything off her' Donnie said, puzzled.

'Why would you smell anything off her, Dunky was using a metaphor, he disnae mean that she is a Vindaloo, that's a metaphor' I said.

Charlie said 'so, if a Vindaloo is a metaphor does that mean that it isnae a curry? Is Chicken Tandoori a metaphor as well because that disnae exactly smell or taste like a curry does it?'

Dunky then laughed and asked Charlie 'Do you not even know what a metaphor is? Ya eejit'

I ignored Dunky's jibe, I was sober them three were drunk. Donnie and Charlie didn't ignore it. He was the drunkest of all of them.

'I'm no' sure what a metaphor is' Donnie said, 'I think it means an example or something but that doesn't make me an eejit'

Charlie then realised that Dunky had been calling his intelligence into question, again. Charlie tended to over react when people did that, any people.

'I haven't got a clue what a metaphor is and I really don't give a monkey's. But I do know what aboot in the balls is, do you? Charlie asked Dunky.

As I said Dunky was also drunk, so the outcome of this was never going to be good. 'I've heard people talk about getting a boot in the balls, I've even gave some people a boot in the balls. I've never had one but, maybe I will meet somebody one of these days that's big enough to give me a boot in the balls. You have had a few, what are they like' Dunky asked Charlie.

They ran at each other and clashed in the middle of the waiting room, blue plastic chairs with black tubular legs went everywhere. The two of them were rolling about on the floor swapping punches. Donnie and I barely managed to drag them apart before three male nurses and two porters barged in and started pulling us all apart. Donnie swung a punch at one of the nurses and I thought 'this is not good'

Surprisingly I managed to stop Donnie throwing any more punches, even more surprisingly the porters and nurses managed to separate Dunky and Charlie before they did any more damage to either themselves or the fixtures and fittings. We were all ejected from the hospital it was only following fifteen minutes of pleading and promising to name my son after the charge nurse that he let me back in. Charlie started arguing again insisting that he should also stay, I suggested to the charge nurse that he should call the police to come with a Black Maria and lift the three of them. They were obviously thugs and had no place in a maternity ward. When he asked me how I knew them, I told him that I didn't, they were three drunken bums that had wandered in off the street. Charlie laughed and told me to phone him with any news or at least phone his neighbour who was happy to take messages apparently.

It was seven o'clock in the morning when the wee nurse from Zimbabwe came and woke me up.

'You are wanted' she said, shaking my shoulder. I had made myself as comfortable as it is possible to be in a hospital waiting room, by lying on the floor.

I had been asleep for all of three hours so I was a little bit disorientated.

'Sorry hen, I'm happily married, you could give Dunky a shout' I mumbled.

She laughed loudly, startling me into sitting up. 'You are not wanted by me, you are wanted by midwife, now very quick' she said with a lovely toothy grin.

'Is she nice looking?' I asked wiping the sleep from my eyes and stretching, before getting to my feet.

'Who?' she asked, bewildered.

'The midwife' I grinned.

She laughed out loud again 'He is a very handsome midwife, but maybe you right he might want you' She giggled and grinned.

Patricia was already taking healthy big gulps of gas and air by the time they had me wrapped up in one of those big green gowns and put a mask and some gloves on me. I felt as if I was going to be doing the operation myself.

I took her hand and she smiled at me briefly and then grimaced as another contraction hit her.

She started to cry 'Danny this is sore'

'I read somewhere that it isnae any worth than toothache' I said in a misguided attempt at humour.

She crushed my fingers 'It's really sore Danny I'm no' kidding on'

I stroked her hair which by now was soaked with sweat, 'I know baby, but it will be over soon' I said kissing her on the forehead through the mask. 'Take some more of that gas and air, I think its laughing gas' I said and squeezed her fingers a bit tighter.

'Aagh' she said as yet another wave of pain overtook her 'It's not fucking making me laugh' she said.

Then it all happened very quickly, one minute the midwife is saying 'Breathe Mrs McAllister, the next he is saying 'Come on give us one pig bush, babies head is out, let's push those big shoulders out' and she did, with an almighty Aagh she gripped my hand, her nails almost drew blood from my palm, she gripped me so tightly. It was quite sore, and you didn't hear me whinging.

Then I heard a baby cry somewhere, for a fraction of a second I was disorientated. I looked round to see if somebody had brought a baby in, then noticed the midwife wrapping a bundle in a white cloth and placing it on Patricia's chest.

'You have a very healthy and handsome boy Mrs McAllister' the midwife said 'and so do you, Danny' he said to me with a wink that got the wee nurse laughing again.

I was mesmerised I stood and stared. It was the most beautiful of all things. Tears streamed down my face. I knew what people meant when they said their heart was bursting with pride. I reached out a hand tentatively and touched his cheek. It was like a little downy peach, he was so soft so fragile looking. He was so amazingly incredibly wonderfully beautiful, he was my son. Patricia smiled at me, my heart was bursting and some more tears bubbled to the surface. I had never believed in tears of joy until that day. She pulled me closer and said 'Look at him Danny, he looks exactly like you' that worried me because to me, he looked more like Winston Churchill but I took her word for it. It was the wrong place and time to get into an argument. The nurse shooed me out of the room, they had things to take care of that I didn't need to be there for she said.

The adrenalin rushed through me; I was desperate to tell somebody. The most incredible amazing thing in the world had happened and nobody knew about it but Patricia and me. My son was born. I said it out loud 'I have a son' I said it again 'I have a son there was nobody there to hear me but it didn't matter, I had a son. So did Patricia if you think about it. I told an old dear that was standing outside having a fag; she must have been in her fifties at least. When I called out to her that I was a daddy, I had a wee boy. She said 'Well done son, was it sore?' The cheeky old boot. Anyway, what the hell was she doing standing about outside the maternity ward in a scabby housecoat and a roll up in her mouth, reliving the good old days?

I ran all the way down to Govan Cross before I spotted a phone box. There was an old boy in it, I waited for him to finish and ruffled his bunnet when he came out and told him my good news. 'That's great son. I hope it turns out better than that wee bastard of mine, four years since I have seen him, four bloody years, and he thinks being in and out of Barlinnie is a bloody excuse. Good for nothing wee bastard that he is, just like his maw. I could only shake my head, what was the matter with these people, miserable old bastards everywhere I looked. I canny see Disney ever wanting to make a feel good movie about Govan, I thought to myself.

But the sour faced old shites couldn't spoil my mood. I found a two bob in my pocket and I phoned my ma, it was a Saturday morning so she was in. 'It's a boy' I screamed down the phone. I waited for her reaction with bated breath. 'Who is this?' she asked. It wasn't actually her that asked that, it was a wee German sounding woman. I must have dialled the wrong number.

I had no change left, I had a fifty pence piece but no ten pence's, so I went in to a wee corner shop and asked for change.

It was an Asian guy serving 'No, I am not giving any change. Because bloody phone bloody box is outside my shop, doesn't mean I am made of change. Bloody BT ask them for change why bloody don't you' I wasn't even going to let this cheeky shite spoil my day 'Listen pal, my wife had a wee boy this morning, I need some ten pence's so I can phone my ma and my brothers and tell them the good news' I told him grinning from ear to ear, and it worked to a certain extent.

Because he grinned back at me and shook my hand 'You are a very lucky bastard' he said 'my useless bastard wife had three daughters and now I will be poor for life, I will probably be buried in my back court as a pauper'

'That's hard cheese pal, it really is' I commiserated 'How about those ten pence's then' I enquired holding up my fifty pence piece.

'Naw' he said 'do you still feel lucky?' he asked grinning again.

'You are luckier than you think' I said to him. He looked puzzled so I explained why he was lucky.

'Look how close you are to the hospital, the ambulance should only take about 3 minutes to get here when I batter your melt in' I said. He had succeeded in bursting my bubble the wee twat. I was still lucky because although I swung at him I missed and as I missed him on the way back as well, a woman behind me in the queue said 'Here son, there's two bob, you can owe me it go and phone your ma, she will be delighted. And don't be too angry at this wee jobby behind the counter, he really is an unlucky wee bastard. Not only did his wife give him three daughters, two of them were after his vasectomy' She and I both laughed, the old Asian guy not so much.

This was my ma's tenth grandchild but she still managed to convey all of her pride and excitement for me when I gave her the news she said 'Danny that's absolutely wonderful son you're going to be a great daddy, is Patricia okay?' I let her know that Patricia was great but very tired and that the baby had all of his fingers and toes and everything was absolutely hunky dory with him. She told me that her and my da would be down the masonic club in Rutland Crescent at the toll by lunchtime, there was some sort of do on, so she would see me in there if I liked and she would get my da to buy me a pint.

She also asked if Patricia needed anything taking up to the hospital because she would be going along this afternoon to see the baby.

I went back along to the hospital to check everything was okay before I went anywhere else. Patricia was sitting up a cup of tea and some toast, but her head was nodding even as she was trying to chew the toast. The nurse advised that it would be best if I buggered off somewhere and wet the baby's head and left Patricia to have a good sleep. To her credit she smiled and said I will, when I asked her who would look after my son while Patricia slept if I wasn't there.

I wondered why I had no feelings of tiredness at all as I sauntered along Govan road. It was almost eleven am and I had decided to go along to the masonic hall as my ma suggested, it should be open by the time I get there.

I walked the length of Govan road from the Southern General Hospital maternity ward to the Paisley Road toll. A walk of perhaps three miles, and I didn't feel my feet contact the ground once. I was walking on air; I felt ten feet tall and indestructible. I had a son. I know people have had children since the dawn of time, but this was different, this was *my* flesh, *my* blood, *my* son.

My ma and da got off a bus outside the hall, coincidentally timed with my arrival on foot. My ma cuddled me, my da shook my hand and told me that he was really happy that I was going to experience all the shit that he had had to and that my troubles were about to begin. Maybe he was right, but I felt as if it was my life that was about to begin. Donnie Dunky and Charlie all arrived with their women shortly after I did. Dunky had Helen with him, so obviously he didn't always have a curry at the weekend.

The function that was on was 'games day' it was a charity event where they held one day competitions in snooker, pool, dominoes and darts. The four pub disciplines in which the McAllister's all excelled, if only there had been a card school, it could well have been the perfect day. I didn't perform all that well in any of them, I couldn't concentrate. My son's face and little fingers and little toes were imbedded in my mind and there was no way I could think of anything but him.

The tiredness I was expecting earlier in the day caught up with me at about six o'clock when we all went back to my ma's for something to eat. Or maybe it was down to the ten pints of lager and six glasses of Bacardi that people bought me to 'wet the baby's head' that I was spark out on the couch by ten past six. Visiting was between seven and eight, I missed it, Patricia, understandably, was not chuffed with me at all.

'So we didn't matter to you then' she accused me. I looked at her and smiled.

'It's because I care about you that I wasn't here last night at visiting time' I smiled again.

'Okay, tell me Danny, I canny wait to hear this one.' She said with undisguised cynicism.

'Right, gonny think about it.' I said beginning my tale 'I phoned my ma to tell her about you and....' I hesitated 'We haven't decided on his name' I said.

'We can do that in a minute or two Danny. Don't try and change the subject, tell me how you getting steaming yesterday and ignoring your wife and new born son, was because you care about us'

‘I phoned my ma, she wisnae in. I went down the club to tell her. People kept buying me drinks, and toasting you and the baby's health. I toasted with them and that proves that I care. So what will we call him’ I said in a single breath.

She looked at me appraisingly and let my absence the previous night go, I was very proud that in the short time we had been married that she had learned it was sometimes better to ignore my idiocy than fight it.

‘What about John Paul?’ I suggested.

‘Why’ she asked.

‘Pope John Paul is coming to Bellahouston Park shortly, that’s a momentous occasion. A world leader coming to Glasgow, that disnae happens every day.’ I suggested.

‘Don’t be ridiculous, what if Ghandi was visiting Glasgow would you want to call him Mahatma Coat’

I smiled ‘His name is just Mahatma’ I said

She looked at me as if I was trying to trick her, ‘My Granda said his name was mahatmamacoat. Anyway my granny and granda would never talk to us again if we called him after the pope; they are in the orange lodge and everything. They would go mental, so would my ma probably’ Patricia said.

‘They will get used to it’ I said ‘My ma is a catholic she would love it’ I bristled and got ready to argue, I don’t like being told what I can and can’t do. Particularly in this case as it looked like it was only to suit somebody’s idiotic and petty prejudices.

‘But I don’t want to either’ Patricia said sitting up in bed and folding her arms across her chest.

‘Why not?’ I asked warily, determined that if her dislike of the name was about religion or pandering to the bigots in her family then it was going to be a fight, maternity ward or not.

‘I don’t like it, I was in the orange walk when I was a wee lassie as well, but I couldn’t give monkeys about it now’ she said with derision. ‘Anyway you are a Rangers supporter, so why would you want to call him a catholic name; no we will call him Patrick instead’

I looked at her quizzically. ‘What?’ She asked.

‘Where did Patrick come from?’ I asked, ‘Who is Patrick, anyway’

‘Me’ she said, ‘We can call our son after me, and Patricia is the women’s version of Patrick. So for a wee change we can call our first son after his mother instead of after his father’

‘That’s not a bad idea hen. Right that’s agreed. Paddy it is!’ I said.

‘Patrick, or maybe even at if you want but not Paddy’ She said with feeling.

So that was it decided Patrick McAllister, a fine and noble name. As far as I had heard Saint Patrick was a Scotsman by birth and the fact that he was the patron saint of Ireland should keep both my ma and da happy because their families came from Ireland originally. I suggested to Patricia that we should give him the middle name Aloysius because that was my da’s middle name. Until I mentioned it to my ma, who told me not to be stupid, my da never had a middle name so he occasionally pretended that he had and that for a laugh when he was drunk and that it was Aloysius. I thought that was quite funny so in an act of respect to my da, when I went to register wee paddy, I registered him as Patrick Aloysius McAllister.

Patricia Eileen McAllister went ape shit on me. Apparently in her opinion, registering my son's birth was no reason to go and get rat arsed drunk with Charlie and ruin our son's entire life by giving him a bloody stupid middle name. She was unimpressed with my opinion that Aloysius was not a stupid name. She was equally unimpressed when I told her that I had looked it up in the library and it meant 'fame and war. In fact she swore at me and screamed at me 'What does that mean, fame and war. Why did you not call him battle of bloody Hastings?' she asked sarcastically.

Wow they hormones must still be doing her head in I supposed. She would calm down at some point about the wee faux pas with the name I reckoned. I'm still waiting.

Our house wasn't deemed warm enough or cosy enough to bring a baby home to, so I had to dismantle the cot and rebuild it in Patricia's ma's house. That was where we were going to from the hospital. It was a cold morning when I went to collect Patricia from the hospital I walked down from Pollokshields to the hospital. We would be getting a taxi back home so I couldn't afford to waste money on bus fares on the way down there. A nurse pushed Patricia in a wheelchair to the front door of the maternity unit and another one carried Patrick in her arms. This was hospital policy apparently which seemed strange to me, Patricia was perfectly capable of walking and I was well able to carry a seven and a half pound baby. But no, they waited until the taxi came helped Patricia into it and then placed Patrick in her arms. That was two nurses for half an hour doing nothing, what a waste of their precious time. I hoped they weren't needed elsewhere. Or maybe they were moving about in pairs in case Dunky came back.

We got him home safely despite the fact that there were no nurses to help us up four flights of stairs into Patricia's ma's house. We put him in his cot and I stared at him for three hours until he woke up and wanted fed. I fed him, changed his nappy, marvelling at his wee tiny yellow jobbies, burped him and put him back in his cot. Then I stared at him for another three hours before doing the same thing again. When he was in a particularly deep sleep, I would prod him frequently to make sure he was breathing. Patricia eventually got fed up with this and told me to leave him alone. So I started prodding him when she wasn't looking.

We spent a couple of days in her ma's, it was fine, no real problems. But neither of us wanted to be there, we had our own house next door. It wasn't that cold, okay we couldn't run the electric fire all the time but we could wrap up well enough including Patrick. When he got a wee tiny cold a few days later Patricia's ma and my ma looked at us accusingly, I told them both to keep their noses out of our business. He was fine it was only a wee cold and a bit of the sniffles. Anyway summer was on its way and once I found a job we could afford to heat the place a bit better.

We did have one of those portable calor gas heaters that you could wheel from room to room. But the only place that sold the big canisters of gas was a garage across from the Plaza ballroom at Eglinton Toll. So it meant I had to carry it on my shoulder all the way back from there. It was easy enough walking there with the empty one but carrying a full one back was murder. It took at least an hour because I had to keep stopping and putting it down for a rest, and each time I put it down it was harder to get it back on my shoulder.

Against Patricia's wishes I started using Patrick's pram to transport the gas cylinder back and forward. It was against her wishes because it was one of our very few possessions that she loved; it was a high pram with a blue cord cloth. My ma had bought it for us, well she gave us the money to go and buy it. So it was Patricia's pride and joy. Which was fair enough but those cylinders were bloody heavy, so I used it. It was quite funny when some of our neighbours would see me walking along McCulloch Street pushing the pram and come over saying 'Oh is that wee paddy, how is he getting on?' only to reach me and discover a 12.5 kg gas container. I would give various responses like 'We swapped him for a bottle of gas' or 'I am not sure who he looks like now, what do you think' or even 'He's getting quite heavy, and blue', or sometimes 'He's underneath that gas bottle you know, he's getting right strong'

I had to stop using it after a couple of months because two wee rat faced bastards tried to steal it from the garage. I was inside paying for the gas and the pram was sitting beside the cage they keep the gas bottles in, I had loaded a bottle in it and went in to pay for the gas. When I came back out there was no pram. I have to admit my bowels quivered, there was no way I was going home to tell Patricia her pride and joy was gone. I raced out of the garage forecourt and spotted the two wee rat faced bastards running down Eglinton Street, one of them pushing the pram. I sprinted after them I chased them for almost half a mile till they reached the County Bingo hall and spotted me behind them. I had almost caught up and couldn't have been more than fifty yards behind them. They must have seen the look on my face because they panicked and pushed the pram onto the road. I stopped running and screamed, my hands coming up to my face. A bus was headed straight for the pram. I don't know if he saw me or heard me scream but he swerved to avoid the pram and had a minor collision with a Ford Fiesta.

The bus driver jumped out of his cab and sprinted to the pram, I got there a hair's breadth before him.

'Is the bairn alright' He asked struggling for breath.

'What bairn' I asked almost shitting myself and looking at the Ford Fiesta, 'was there a wean in that car'

'The bairn in the pram you half-wit' he said still wheezing and bent over with his hands on his knees.

'This bairn?' I asked throwing back the top cover and revealing the gas bottle with and inappropriate flourish and an equally inappropriate laugh.

'You dickhead' he called me 'I have got about twenty passengers on this bus I could have killed them if I had swerved and crashed into a wall trying to avoid your fuckin pram' he said.

'You could also have killed them if you had hit the pram and the gas bottle then blew up you wanker' I said, tucking the gas bottle in with a wee pat and a smile and bumping the pram back up on to the pavement. He was lucky really, if I hadn't been so relieved at the pram escaping unscathed, I could have taken exception to him calling me a dickhead. So he had a lucky escape in more ways than one. With Patricia's hormones still going mental, I decided that I better not tell her about my adventure. There's no point in inviting trouble is there?

Chapter Twenty seven. We can't keep on being skint. Do something, anything.

'Danny, you really need to do something, we can't keep on being skint like this' Patricia said to me.

I was lying on my back on the bed in our kitchen with Patrick in my hands above me, pulling him down to my face kissing him and then pushing him back up in the air again. He loved it, he was giggling like mad. He loved it so much he occasionally thanked me by being sick in my face, sometimes scoring a direct hit into my mouth. This was an occasion of a direct hit.

Patricia burst out laughing and said 'How stupid are you, he does that nearly every time and you still keep throwing him up and down like that. You deserve all you get'

I put him on the bed and went to the sink to wash my mouth out. 'Don't leave him on the bed like that he's nearly crawling' She shouted at me but didn't bother racing to the rescue.

'No he isnae' I said 'he's only four months old, he canny crawl yet' Only to turn round and see him turn on to his belly grab a hold of the candlewick, kick his wee legs as hard as he could and try to pull himself along. He succeeded in moving about a foot towards the edge of the bed. I leapt on to the bed and started tickling him. 'You little shit why are you making out that your daddies a liar, when did you start doing this?' I asked him while kissing his belly and making him laugh again. I could listen to him laugh forever it was the sweetest sound in the world.

'He was doing it last night, when you were at the Quaich with your brothers. Spending whatever money we had left' she said, opening the fridge probably so I could see how empty it was.

'Why do you do this?' I asked, 'you know I never spent any money last night because I didnae have any money to spend. Charlie and Dunky bought me a couple of pints and Donnie gave me couple of his roll ups. What do you think I should do? Should I go down there and say, listen boys don't buy me a pint gonny gimme the money instead, Patricia canny afford to buy her make-up this week?'

'That's terrible why would you say that to me, I don't want to buy make up, when do I ever buy anything for me, ever?' I want to buy food for us and maybe a fuckin toilet roll, a bottle of bleach or maybe luxuries like bread and fuckin milk' she shouted at me.

Patrick squealed at the sudden noise and started crying, loudly. If I had been a little more mature I would have realised that she was shouting at our circumstance rather than directly at me. But I wasn't.

'Look what you have done now you stupid cow, he was all happy and now he's screaming blue murder. Why is it only my fault we're skint? You know I want to work, you know I'm always out looking for a job any job; I would empty the bins and sweep the street if I got the chance. In fact I put my name down with the cleansing months ago. Why don't you get off your arse and go back to work in the bingo or get a cleaning job with your ma or something, instead of blaming me' I ranted all the time upsetting Patrick more, holding him in my arms and rocking him in an attempt to soothe him, it wasn't really working, not while I was screaming at his mother at the same time anyway.

If Patricia had been a bit more mature she would have realised that I wasn't screaming at her. I was screaming with frustration at the world, I wanted to work, I needed to work, and I was willing to work. So why couldn't I get a bloody job. But she wasn't very mature either.

'All right, I will get a job if you canny manage to' she said and stormed out. It was like a knife in my heart, did she know that she was attacking my manhood, did she even care? She was hitting out at me when I was already down and there wasn't very much lower that I could go. But with hindsight me saying that she only wanted money for makeup was also a low blow, I suppose.

She was gone for hours, for most of the day and evening in fact. I was alternately fuming and panicking. I was raging that she should criticise me for not working when she knew how desperate I was for a job, and I was panicking because what if she had left me, for good?

She came in at about nine o'clock, drunk, carrying a plastic carrier bag.

I again let my lack of maturity take control 'Where the fuck have you been until this time of night?' I asked with menace.

'In the pub, my pals were buying me drink, so I haven't spent a penny' she started laughing 'I don't mean spending a penny in like doing a pee. Because I have done a pee but I haven't spent a penny in money if you know what I mean' I should have been able to laugh along with her but I wasn't.

'Where is my baby, has he missed his mammy' she slurred as she got to her feet and staggered towards the kitchen, door closed to prevent her going through to the kitchen.

'He's sleeping, where did you think he would be at this time of night' I barked at her, giving no space at the front of my mind to the memory of me waking him up at two in the morning the night before just so I could hear him giggle when I tickled him.

She looked at the sunburst clock on the wall and said 'It's nine o'clock Danny the fanny, that's no late is it? You stay out to after one when your 'pals' buy you a drink or three don't you. Why am I no' allowed to do that, eh Danny the fanny eh?'

‘But it’s no’ my pals I’m out with it’s my brothers’ was my pathetic poorly thought through response.

‘Oh that’s right, Danny’s perfect brothers the good guys. The McAllister boys from Cessnock Street, the Paisley road Wild West gang of eejits. Youse sound like something from Bonanza, like some gang of cowboys with white hats on’ she burst out laughing ‘and that’s what youse are, really, a bunch of useless cowboys’ she continued to laugh.

I pushed past her, fed up of being in the same room with her when she was this drunk and getting annoyed and angry. I didn’t mean for her to fall, I didn’t push her, I pushed past her.

‘You pushed me’ she shouted at me as she struggled to get back to her feet, when I pushed past her she had fallen down on the armchair and had then slipped off it and landed on her arse on the floor. So she was now trying to push herself back up onto the armchair as she shouted at me.

‘No I didnae, you fell on your own arse you’re that drunk. I am surprised you managed to walk home, you’re that pissed’ I said unsympathetically.

She burst into sobs ‘Danny McAllister you pushed me, I am your wife and Patricks father, I mean Patricks mother, you are his father and you pushed me down on the floor how could you? You are supposed to love me you bastard’ she sobbed and then continued asking me why and how could I hit her like that. Then she degenerated into unintelligible sobbing which still had words mingled in but they were completely unfathomable. I sat on the floor beside her and put my arm round her shoulder pulling her head on to my shoulder.

'I didnae push you, I was trying to get past you and you were staggering and you fell on the chair and bounced off onto your arse. Nobody pushed you; you're just a wee bit drunk baby.' I hugged her a bit closer as she continued to sob. Snatches of her sobbing were discernible 'you pushed me' I'm no drunk' 'I'm Paddy's mammy' 'I'm not your baby' 'you're a liar'.

Her sobs stopped after a few minutes not because she was finished feeling sorry for herself but because she had fallen asleep. So much for her not being drunk, she was out for the count.

I lifted her and carried her ben to the kitchen to put her to bed. Why is she so much heavier to carry when she is asleep than she is when she is awake? When she is sober and awake I can throw her over my shoulder and carry her about no problem. But drunk and asleep she weighs a ton, why is that?

I flopped her out of my arms and onto the bed and start to undress her; Shoes first and then her jeans, her very tight jeans. I am pulling and hauling at them and have almost got them down past her knees when she sits up and says 'I don't want to make love, you pushed me, and I'm not your baby any more' and then lies back down asleep again before her head touched the pillow. I eventually get her stripped down to her underwear and pull a nightgown over her head. I was very tempted to give her a big love bite on her neck to embarrass her the next day but I didn't.

Patricia at the best of times likes at least three quarters of the bed and the entire quilt, when drunk she wants all of the bed and none of the quilt. Consequently I get almost no sleep when she is drunk and sleeping. I sometimes slip through to sleep on the couch under these circumstances but didn't this time, because I was feeling a bit guilty about her falling. While she was asleep and snoring her little ladylike snore, and everything was quiet and there was nobody awake but me. I couldn't quite convince myself that I hadn't pushed her. I spent an almost sleepless night questioning myself, at one point I woke Patrick up to ask him if he thought I pushed his ma. He didn't know. Or if he did have an opinion on the matter he wasn't telling me.

I fell asleep at about six o'clock and woke up at nine o'clock. Patricia was still spark out but not for long. I jumped on the bed landing on all fours, my hands at either side of her head and my knees at either side of her waist.

'Do you want some tea and toast' I asked her pushing my hands up and down on the mattress and making her head bounce on the pillow.

'Aagh, fuck off danny let me sleep' she said delicately, pulling the quilt back over her head.

I pulled it back down 'it's eleven o'clock' I said.

'So what' she responded 'what have I got to get up for'

'My ma and Darlene are coming up today' I informed her cheerily.

'What the hell for and when did you find that out' she asked pushing the quilt down and looking at me with suspicion.

'About half an hour ago, when I phoned and asked my ma for a wee tap just a few quid to keep us going. She told me Darlene was through from Coventry and had a new car and that she would give my ma a wee run up to see us' I said kissing her on the lips and shaking her head from side to side with my hands. She didn't like that, not at all.

‘Aagh’ she said pushing me off her roughly and attempting to swing her legs round and sit up. She shouldn’t have tried to do that so quickly it hurt her head. ‘When will they be up?’ she asked hanging her head and running her fingers through her hair, without much success it must be said.

‘I need to have a bath; I’ll take Patrick in with me. You iron his wee blue stripy suit that your ma gave him and put it on him and make sure the blankets on his pram are spotless, you know what Darlene is like she will be sticking her beak in everywhere, what time are they coming?’

‘Not for ages yet why don’t you lie down and let me wake you up slowly and gently’ I said slipping my hands round her waist and working my way up wards. Before she could chastise me and slap me somebody rattled the letter box. Patricia whispered to me ‘If that’s them I will kill you stone dead. In fact if that’s them tell them to piss off and come back in an hour, they canny turn up out of the blue uninvited or unannounced’

‘Are you mental? I’m no’ telling my ma to piss off, I’ll tell Darlene to piss off but no’ my ma. Anyway I invited them and if you want them announced I will announce them’ I said smiling as I went to answer the door.

Charlie went past me and into the kitchen before I could stop him. ‘Are you not up yet you lazy bastard’ He asked Patricia.

‘Danny tell your stupid brother to piss off I need to go for a bath before your ma comes up’ she said quickly wrapping the candlewick from the bottom of the bed round her as she still only had her underwear on pushing past him.

Do you want me to wash your back?" he asked her and then turned to me 'What's my ma coming up for'

I looked at him with wonder 'Gonny no' sexually harass my wife when I am standing right here in front of you. I phoned her for a tap and because Darlene was through with her new motor she decided she would just bring it up to me' I said

'I wisnae sexually harassing her I was offering to wash her back, if I was sexually harassing her I would have offered to wash her front. If you need a tap you should have phoned me. I've had the phone put in and you know how much my ma moans at you when you tap her. You are supposed to be the clever one with loads of money; it's me that's supposed to be stupid and skint'

"You do okay with the first part' I responded, not really being in the mood for Charlie's condescension. But as usual he surprised me.

'I will let that go Danny, because you're my brother and I know that you know that I'm not really stupid' he then went into his pocket took out some money and handed me £40. 'Don't tell anybody I gave you that, I try to keep my charity work secret' he said with a grin.

I balled up the money and threw it at him 'Stick it up your arse' were my heartfelt words of thanks.

'Jesus Christ Danny, what's up with you? When did you lose your fucking sense of humour?' he said angrily stooping to pick the money up and pushing it into my trouser pocket. 'Take a joke man, it's not any worse than you would do to me' I didn't take the money out of my pocket but neither was I bursting into songs of praise for him.

'It isnae funny Charlie, Patricia is giving me grief big style, I canny keep tapping money and taking hand outs from you and Dunky whenever I want a pint, it's out of order' I said coming as close as I could to an apology.

'The day will come Danny, when you are doing the giving, don't worry about that'

I was surprised that he seemed to believe that, it certainly wasn't something that I believed. I felt two inches tall, I was twenty years of age and here was my younger brother giving me hand outs (again) to save me from tapping my ma for money. How did it come to this, I was a qualified engineer and I had loads of certificates and o'levels. But then as Charlie had said to me once before, 'take your certificates and your o-levels into the co-op and see how many blocks of cheese you get for them'

'I canny hang about Danny; tell my ma I will see her tomorrow. I've got some news for her, Iris is pregnant again, but don't tell her I want to tell her' he said with a big grin, clearly trying to reduce the tension or to get me smiling or both.

'Iris is pregnant but she disnae know it?' I asked slightly bewildered, and he just stared at me until I got it 'aw you mean don't tell my ma that Iris is pregnant don't you?' I grinned sarcastically as if I had known all along and was trying to be funny.

'What was he wanting this time, has nobody told him that he doesn't live here anymore, he lives in the Gorbals now?' Patricia asked as she came out of the bathroom wrapping her hair in a towel, how do they manage to make that Turban thing by the way? That never works for me.

'Nothing' I said

'Nothing? She asked her voice dripping with sarcasm and suspicion.

'Iris is pregnant again and he lent me £40. Apart from that nothing' I said.

'Well that's no nothing, that's quite a big thing actually' she said.

'I've tapped him and for a lot more than that before?' I said quizzically.

'No' you tapping him you eejit, Iris being pregnant again is a big thing' she said with exasperation.

I grinned and responded 'You're no kidding that's a big thing, she was bloody huge with wee Charlie' I slipped out the front door before she could berate me for taking the piss.

I only went out for some rolls and cold meat and maybe a packet of Rich tea or something. I wouldn't have to tap my ma now and I could give her a cup of tea and something to eat now, so it might be possible to hide how skint we were and how hard we were finding things.

'You'se don't like a lot of furniture or ornaments or anything do you'se' Darlene asked looking around the living room 'what is it the call that again, miniaturist?'

'No its minimalism, miniaturist is what they done to your brain when you were born, you half-wit. Where did you get the car' I asked her, I was looking out my living room window at a cracking wee yellow convertible MG car with the roof down. This was probably why my ma was at my house with Darlene, she was getting a taste for fancy cars. She had gone down to Redcar a year or two previously in a convertible, with her sunglasses and headscarf on. I am sure she felt like Debbie Reynolds or something.

'It's mine' Darlene said, cagily.

'Yours a loan of, or yours to keep, or yours to hide from the polis?' I asked, maybe she thinks I have forgot what a toerag her man was.

'I have it out on a test run from a garage in Coventry, big John does some work for the guy that owns the garage. Is that my old couch?' She asked, skilfully changing the subject.

'No your couch was a hell of a lot darker than that Darlene' my ma said running her hand across the back of it.

'No Mrs McAllister it is Darlene's couch, I gave it a good clean with that 1001 carpet shampoo stuff and it came up that lovely pale blue, I had thought it was navy blue at first, or black' Patricia said, I like to think she was innocent and didn't realise she was insulting Darlene. I do like to think that but I don't believe it.

'It wisnae black when I gave you it, but Danny always was a manky wee tramp, he's probably been lying about on it all day. Since he's no' got a job. That's why it's turned black.' Darlene said haughtily.

'Maybe it was black because that was the same as every other minging thing that was in your house, including you and your weans' bogging necks. And by the way, you never 'gave' us it you abandoned it when you did a moonlight flit. So maybe you want to be careful before you open that stupid mouth of yours and stick both feet in it' I said with a sarcastic threatening smile.

'Gonny tell him to shut it ma' Was Darlene's intellectual response.

'*Gonny tell him to shut it mammy'* said in a childish screechy voice was my much more mature response to her.

'Why don't both of you'se just grow up or shut up? Are you putting the kettle on Patricia hen, my throats parched' my ma said. I prodded Darlene in the side with my elbow as I passed her on my way to the kitchen to make the tea.

'Gonny tell him' she screeched.

I said 'Darlene why don't you grow up, you're nearly twenty eight for god's sake'

I closed the living room so I barely heard her screaming at my ma 'Gonny tell him I'm only twenty six' she screeched.

'Are you gonny wash they plates with cold water and no Squeezy liquid' Darlene asked Patricia, condescendingly. We had finished our cups of teas and rolls and corned beef, so Patricia was rinsing the cups and plates.

'She's rinsing your slabbers off them, so the wean canny catch any of your bacteria off them and I'll wash them later when we put the immersion heater on and there is hot water. In the meantime I will just keep the wean away from them, we wouldn't want him to catch anything would we' I replied scathingly.

'You cheeky besom I don't have any bacteria or whatever you said, I have just had a check-up and the only thing wrong with me is that I have acute angina. Well, that's what it sounded like my gynaecologist said' Darlene said with a huge screeching laugh. 'Acute angina, do you get it?' she asked screeching again and again.

'Aye I get it you fanny' I whispered so my ma wouldn't hear me.

'I heard that Daniel, don't be disgusting' my ma said.

We managed to get rid of them without me smacking Darlene one on the kisser and then we stood at the window watching her trying to make a big deal out of fixing her head scarf and her lipstick in the car mirror. My ma saw me standing there and motioned me to come over to her, so I opened the window and hopped out into the garden and went over to my ma, much to Patricia's disgust, she was forever moaning at me for using the window as the front door.

'Daniel do you think I could learn to drive' my ma asked me.

I bent into the car and kissed her on the cheek and said 'you can do absolutely anything you want ma, I mean look at Darlene'

Darlene smiled and said 'Aye ma if I can learn to drive anybody can'

I looked at Darlene and said 'I actually meant that the very fact you learned to walk and talk means that absolutely anything is possible. The way I look at it sweetheart you're only twenty eight, you've still got lots of time to learn how to think as well. Go for it ma, if you fancy it then why not, Darlene and Charlie have passed their driving tests, seriously how hard can it be' I gave her another kiss and pre-empted Darlene's whinging by giving her a kiss as well and teller her she knows I'm only joking. As if.

In fact my ma made me think that if could learn to drive I might find it much easier to get a job. But how would I get the money for driving lessons they were a tenner a pop. We could live off a tenner a week in fact most weeks we did live off less than a tenner. Driving would have to stay a dream for a wee while I thought, and I was right.

'Okay I'm in' I said to Charlie as soon as I saw him next. This happened to be in the Quaich bar on the following Tuesday night, darts night.

'In what' he asked, looking at me as if I was stupid. Which I definitely was, for even considering getting into anything dodgy with him.

'The next time you and searcher are on the rob', I will come with you' I told him as if I was bestowing a big favour on him.

'Okay' he responded ' The very first time we need a shitebag that canny drive and that thinks we are thieving bastards, I will come and get you'

'How am I a shitebag? And it was you that told me to stop being so high and mighty and do what I need to do to feed my family'

'I meant con the social, tell them that you and her aren't together anymore. Put your address down as my ma's house. They will give her a Monday book and you will get your own money. You can then claim for furniture, you tell them my ma threw out your bed and your bedding and all the bedroom furniture and they will give you a grant for it. Start trying to think smart for a change, instead of being a good wee boy. You've got a family, do what you need to do.'

'What I need to do is work' I said adamantly.

'Well work then and stop fucking whinging' he said getting up and going to the bar.

He was right I suppose, I was on frequently perched on a high horse like some moral knight. Looking down on everybody else who learned their way around the social security system and made sure they were getting as much as they could possibly get from it, rightly or wrongly. And why shouldn't they? I didn't see any of the royal family nor the politicians going hungry weren't they just exploiting the same system? Although I somehow doubt that Maggie Thatcher had a Monday book.

Dunky came in and dropped his bomb-shell as soon as he sat down 'Helen is six months pregnant' he said, grinning like a demented clown.

Donnie doubted the truthfulness of the statement with some justification if there was an expert on pregnancy in our family it was him he already had five weans 'Six months? And the two of you have just noticed how does that work?'

'How should I know? I'm not a doctor am I? She felt funny and went to the doctors, the next thing is she's told she's six months gone and that's that, what should I do call the Doctor a liar, why would he lie?' Dunky said missing Donnie's point completely, probably because he was already half drunk and he had just arrived.

'Have you been going out with her for six months?' I asked with suspicion in my voice now.

'Aye Danny I have actually, I've been going out with for nearly nine months on and off, and even before I was officially going out with her, I was 'seeing her' once in a while, if you know what I mean' he said starting to get irritated at the inquisition.

'Was she 'seeing' anybody else, like you were?' Charlie chimed in as he put a tray on the table with four pints of lager and four Bacardi and cokes on it.

'Naw she wisnae, she's a nice lassie' Dunky responded getting angrier by the second. Although his anger didn't stop him downing one of the Bacardi and cokes in a single gulp it barely touched the sides.

The other three of us laughed and I voiced what we were all thinking 'If she's a nice lassie why the fuck is she going out with you' to Dunky's credit he laughed it off and we all got down to some serious drinking, we were celebrating the latest McAllister boy to add to the clan. Donnie had more than done his bit; as I mentioned he was up to five kids now. Charlie was percolating his second and I had just produced my first so Dunky was the last of the four of us boys to chip in. Although I do think Donnie had an excellent point when he asked how many kids there might be across England and Wales who might one day come looking for their fathers.

Dunky paled a little at that thought but then brightened up when he remembered that he had almost always told any girls that he went with that his name was Donnie McAllister. Donnie got the last and best laugh I when he said 'What a coincidence I always told them my name was Dunky, and better than that, so did my da'

Which reminded me that my da had told us in one of his drunken moments that there was a definite chance that we had a couple of German half-brothers and sisters, because he had had two German girls on the go at the same time, when he had did his national service in Berlin after the war. He even claimed that he was pretty sure he had married at least one of them, and he thought both of them could have been pregnant when he left. But as they were both on the buxom side he couldn't be sure. I put it down to his imagination and watching too many carry on films. He was a romancer at the best of times, he knew how to tell a tall tale in fact half of the lies he told us weren't true. And if it was true that he had married one of them, then didn't that make his marriage to my ma null and void. This meant that we were all illegitimate, wee bastards in other words. Could all be true I suppose.

The drinking side of the night ended for Dunky when he got thrown out of the Old Toll bar for winching one of the barmaids when she was supposed to be working. Most of the time that wouldn't necessarily get you thrown out of the pub, but since this barmaid was married to the guy who owned the pub, and he was standing right behind her, it didn't go down too well. Some of the punters, clearly hoping for a free pint or at least trying to stay in the owners good books joined in to help throw Dunky out. Had the owner of the pub thrown Dunky out by himself, then that would have been the end of it, we would have laughed and moved on. Dunky knew that the barmaid was married to the owner so he probably deserved to get thrown out and maybe even deserved a bit of a slap. But he didn't deserve three dickheads holding him up so the cow's husband could punch his lights out.

Donnie and Dunky got the jail. Only because Dunky was too drunk to run when the police arrived in a riot van and Donnie refused to stop kicking the owner of the pub in the face. Even when I grabbed him and told him the police had arrived he just told me to beat it, he wisnae finished what he was doing.

Charlie and I bolted and we could both shift a bit even when we were steaming. The three police who even attempted to chase us gave up within a half a mile. We stopped running just when we got to Cessnock Street.

'What now?' I asked him when I had finished being sick into the litter bin on the lamppost next to the zebra crossing at the end of Cessnock street.

Charlie was laughing 'Look at you, you even vomit tidily' I only grinned in response.

'Home, I suppose. Unless you want to wake my ma up for a cup of tea and a piece and sausage' he said.

I considered it 'No, it's a Tuesday night. She will be up at four for her shift in Leverndale and my da will be up at six. What about chapping Searcher or big Boaby up and seeing if they fancy going and doing a wee turn' I said returning to my plan of earlier in the night of getting involved with Charlie and his wee gang to make some money.

'If you wanted to go to jail why did you no' just stay with Donnie and Dunky, they will end up in Orkney street at some point tonight, I guarantee it? How stupid are you. The two of us are miroculous drunk and you want to wake Searcher and big Boaby up to go on the rob. Are you off your head or what?'

'Aye, you're right we shouldn't wake them up that would be stupid. Especially since they aren't even sleeping' I said laughing and pointing behind him at Searcher and Boaby dawdling along the Paisley road as if it was a Sunday afternoon.

‘Are all they polis back there looking for you two?’ Searcher asked as he reached us.

‘Why do you ask?’ Charlie asked back.

‘Well they aren’t looking for us so it must be you’se’ Searcher said with an air of finality.

‘It could be somebody else they are looking for and nothing to do with us’ Boaby offered. All four of us said ‘aye right’ and laughed.

‘Danny wants to go on the rob Searcher, tell him how stupit he is will you please?’ Charlie said sitting down on the edge of the pavement. This must have been further down than he thought because I could hear the thud over Boaby’s laughter and Charlie’s squeal of pain. He would have sat on the wall behind him except boaby had sat there and his fat arse took up most if not all of the available space.

‘Oh you bastart I think I’ve broke my arse’ He squealed out.

‘Well it wouldn’t take much’ I said ‘There was already a big crack in it’ Boaby laughed the other two grimaced, but Boaby was always a good audience.

‘Rob where?’ Searcher asked, never one to shirk a challenge or an opportunity to make money.

‘Let’s do Connals’ I said, pointing at the warehouse half way down Cessnock Street.

‘Naw, you don’t shite in your own nest. We aren’t wee boys any more Danny. When we do a warehouse now we go with a plan and whatever transport we need. And before we go we know what is in it and what we want to take out of it. We also know exactly how much we will get for it and who will be buying it. We don’t just run out with what we can carry and hope for the best. Fucking grow up why don’t you’ Charlie said with exasperation.

I stared at him and continued to stare at him until he made eye contact. 'Fuck you' I said succinctly. He knew it wasn't okay to try and bring me down in front of other people; he stood up ready to fight, albeit rubbing his sore arse, which diminished his gesture a bit. I stood up as well; it had been a couple of years since we had had an actual fight, no holds barred. I was out of practice and hesitant, he was neither.

He launched himself at me but Boaby grabbed the back of his denim jacket before he had got more than a yard closer to me.

'Danny do you remember the very first time we broke into Connals' Boaby asked me as Charlie struggled to free himself and called Boaby a few unpleasant names and threatened him with a few unpleasant things.

'We knocked a load of wine gums' Boaby's eyes lit up with the memory. 'Can none of you remember' he asked looking round at all of us.

'I remember Boaby but that was the second time we robbed it, the first time we took four pallets of milk tray and left ten pallets of *Bells Whisky* or was it *The Famous Grouse* I know it was one of them' I said still keeping an eye on Charlie but he had caught the Boaby bug. Sometimes when Boaby stood and remembered when we were weans it was as if he was actually back there. He stood and looked down at the ground, smiling.

'Aye but the wine gums were the best night ever' he said.

I chuckled and sat down on the wall beside him, he let Charlie go and he sat down as well, without breaking his arse any further.

'Were you there Searcher I canny remember' I said and looked at him.

A big grin appeared on his face and he answered 'Too right I was there that's the night I lost my virginity' All four of us laughed but Charlie took the tone down 'Did your arse bleed much' he asked.

Searcher did the right thing and ignored him 'I remember about half of the warehouse being filled with pallets of wine gums and jelly babies' he started.

Boaby interrupted 'I loved them wine gums'

'We fuckin know' all three of us responded before Searcher got on with his tale.

'You'se all must remember that the other half of the warehouse was filled with all the massive sheets of foam. After we had stuffed my cellar with all the wine gums and jelly babies we were ready to scarper but then wee Georgina Duffy and her pals spotted us and wanted in to see what we were doing, and we let them.' Searcher said.

'Aye I remember' I said 'there were four of them and Boaby and Charlie climbed up onto the pallets of foam and started kicking it all over the place, just showing off. But then Charlie took it too far as usual and started jumping off the rafters and landing on the foam. I was standing watching him, wondering who would get the pleasure of telling my ma that the wee fanny had broken his neck'

Charlie grinned and joined in 'That's right you shat yourself as usual and wouldn't do it. Even Boaby hauled his big fat arse up into the rafters and done it once and peg leg over there even did it when Boaby helped him to get up high enough.

I looked at him and said 'I was too busy trying to get off with wee Georgina Duffy to be bothered with jumping about on cushions like a four year old'

'Ha ha, you weren't any good at that either then, because it was her I humped underneath all them foam sheets when you'se all went away'

I laughed along with them and added 'that wee boot told me she had never done it as well, you must have been her first'

‘Second maybe’ Boaby grinned and blushed.

‘At least third’ Charlie said and lay down on the pavement he was laughing so hard.

‘Wee cow’ I said ‘What was so wrong with me?’

‘I know where she lives, if you want to go and ask her’ Charlie offered ‘Maybe she will let you now’ he added with glee.

‘No’ after you’se three have done her, you must be joking I wouldn’t even go into a toilet after you’se three disease ridden middens I said.

‘There were more than five hundred and twenty wine gums in each box’ Big Boaby commented out of nowhere.

‘It said 600 on the box’ Searcher answered ‘I remember because I sold them to Johnny the Jesuit at the Barra’s and the old shite made me stand and count out a full box to prove it’

‘What makes you think there was only 520 Boaby?’ I naively asked.

‘I never said there were 520 in the box. I said there were more than 520 in the box. My problem is that I canny count past 520’ he answered.

‘What the fuck are you talking about Boaby’ Searcher asked ‘if you can count up to 520 then you can count to whatever you want’

‘I really canny Searcher’ Boaby said with real conviction ‘Because I always fall asleep at 520, always’

We all laughed and Charlie said ‘Come on Danny, this is doing my box in. All this shit only happened about seven or eight years ago and you three are sitting there reminiscing like old men talking about the war. Come on let’s go back to yours and get Patricia up to make us something to eat’

‘I don’t think so’ I said ‘She goes off her nut when I take any of you lot back after the last time when you broke all her ornaments. Let’s go to yours for a change’

‘Is she no’ over that yet, she bears a grudge that lassie so she does. And no you canny come back to mine it’s not even midnight yet. If I go home before twelve o’clock Iris will think I am up to something’ he said and looked at Searcher, with an unspoken but understood question of whether we were going to his house, but he just shook his head.

‘I am going into Connals’ boaby announced.

I laughed as did Charlie, Searcher didn’t he knew that once Boaby decided he was going in then that meant they were both going in. ‘There won’t be any wine gums Boaby, no way will there be any wine gums. You will get us the jail looking for wine gums’

Big Boaby laughed and said ‘We’ve had the jail for less wee man; come on it will be a giggle’

‘If we get the jail, you’re paying the fines big man I mean it’ Searcher said and that was that the decision was made we were going in.

The problem that none of us foresaw or to be honest cared about was that scaling a twenty foot wall onto a factory roof was easier when you were twelve than it was when you were in your twenties. Boaby couldn’t get up on the dyke to get near the wall, Charlie got up as smooth as you like and once on the roof pulled me up. We both then took Searcher’s hands and pulled him up beside us. Charlie smashed a skylight on the roof and we prepared to go in, as this was an unplanned adventure we had to light our lighters to use as torches. This allowed us to see slightly but not very much there were still many more shadows than anything else.

That was probably the reason that Searcher missed the roof beam that Charlie and I had used to drop onto the pallets below us. Searcher unfortunately not only missed using the roof beam he also missed the pallets and fell thirty feet to the concrete floor. Luckily he avoided landing on his bad leg and making it worse. Unluckily he landed on his good leg and broke it.

Charlie thought this was hilarious and burst out laughing and began shouting at Searcher for being a stupid clumsy bastard. Bizarrely Searcher laughed along with him, albeit between screams of pain. He begged us to get him an ambulance.

'Don't be stupid Searcher if we phone an ambulance we will all get the jail' was Charlie's typically unsympathetic response. 'We can pull you back up through the skylight and throw you down the other side of the wall, that way you get to hospital and we don't get caught' He added as a plan.

Searcher looked at me 'Don't let him throw me off that wall Danny, please. He's not joking he will do it'

I grinned at him and said 'We will tell Boaby to catch you'

I don't know if he got three shades paler in his face because his leg was starting to bleed profusely or because he believed we would actually do that to him. I looked at Charlie and I swear he looked like he was trying to work out a way to get searcher to the top of the pallets and back out on to the roof. It didn't matter either way because we heard somebody call 'Who's there' from the other end of the warehouse; it was a watchie, a night watchman.

'Out you go Danny, I will stay with him. Go piss off Patricia will do me in if you get the jail again, she always blames me as it is'

I sat down on the floor beside Searcher 'Bolt Charlie, you are on probation you'll get six months if you get caught. I will get a slap on the wrist or a fine. I've got no previous for breaking and entering you have.' It made sense and Charlie knew it. I boosted him up on to a nearby pallet and away he went.

The watchie might or might not have seen him, as it turned out it didn't matter much.

'Well, well, well. If it isnae Danny McAllister. What brings the brave and bold Danny boy back to Cessnock then? Is Pollokshields too posh for you, have you come to rough it with the Govan boys. Of course you have and here's the proof, you brought your own wee midgie raker with you. And look at that the poor wee soul is broken'

I recognised the whining nasal voice before I saw the pockmarked ugly coupon of Ronnie Watson, my childhood nemesis and constant enemy. I had two choices I could take his torch off of him and stick it up his arse or....

'Ronnie mate how you doing?' I asked him with as much vigour and friendliness as I could manage 'So are you in security now? Smart uniform by the way'

He looked at me with justified and righteous suspicion but seemed to swallow the bait.

'Aye ahm ur actually' he said with a significant amount of pride as he removed imaginary lint from one of his epaulettes. 'I'm in charge of security for this whole factory now' he said beaming.

'Good man, it used to be a big Alsatian' I said facetiously. Why could I never keep my stupid mouth shut?

He squinted at me with more suspicion 'Aye I had that dug for a wee while, but it wouldn't stop biting me on the arse and they took it off me and gave me a bigger torch. What is you'se fucking doing anyway; it's nearly two in the morning. He asked as he shone his bigger torch up and down the length of Searcher's body.

'I'm not doing that much really, other than standing having a gas with you. But I think Searcher might be bleeding to death' I said, dead pan.

He grinned 'You were always the funny one Danny, Charlie thought he was funny, he looked funny that's all' he said. I decided to keep that one in my locker to tell Charlie later.

‘The thing is Ronnie, we need a wee favour. We were having a bit of a giggle over the old days and searcher here decided that he wanted to see if there were any wine gums in here. Like there was that time when we were weans. Do you remember all the weans in the street ended up being sick of wine gums and ended up just pelting them at each other for a laugh’ I said lightly punching Ronnie’s arm to emphasise our camaraderie.

‘The way I remember it was that you’se all ate them until you’se were sick of them and then started pelting me with them and telling me to eat the ones I could catch’ he answered obviously still resentful. Sometimes people need to learn to let go.

‘Aye’ I said ignoring his angst ‘It was always a right good laugh back then wasn’t it. Anyway, Ronnie, we need to get the accident victim an ambulance. I really don’t like how white he is going and to be honest my black suit is in the pawn, so I canny really afford for him to die. Well not until I get my next giro anyway’

Ronnie looked the victim up and down and the looked me up and down and said ‘Fair enough, I will call an ambulance and the polis, it just means you need to get done for burglary but’

‘Whoa hold up Ronnie, if you just open up the roller door over there, I will drag searcher out into the road and we can say he got knocked down or fell off a horse or something, nobody needs to get done, do they?’

‘But what’s in that for me, if I phone the polis and dub you’se two in. I get a pat in the back from the boss and probably an extra tenner in my wages. So why would I help you two get aff scot free, do you think I’m an eejit or something’ he said with cunning and some glee.

‘Here Ronnie, open the fucking door. I think I might be fuckin dying here, whilst you’se two dick about’ searcher said throwing two twenty pound notes at Ronnie’s feet and collapsing on to his back having sat up to throw the money.

Ronnie inspected the notes by the light of his torch and accepted that they were real. 'Fair enough, but when we drag him onto the road you can come back in and at least I caught one burglar'

'No, I need to stay with him while you phone an ambulance or maybe somebody will run over him and how daft would that make us feel' I said out loud 'Don't be so fuckin stupit you absolute moron' I said in my head.

'Aye all right then but just because we were all good muckers when we were wee' he said strolling away towards the button that raised the warehouse door and the office that contained the phones.

My ma would have been proud of me, the way I managed to hold my tongue and not blurt out that 'good muckers' didn't normally slash each other or put each other in a baseball bat induced coma. Instead I bit my tongue, grabbed Searcher by the shoulders and started dragging him towards the door. Before it was even open boaby ducked under it and saw Searcher in clear pain and discomfort.

'What happened here Danny was this anything to do with that wee snivelling bastart' Boaby asked pointing at and moving towards Ronnie.

'Don't even think about it retard, I'll set the dug on you' Ronnie said as he ducked into the office and locked the door behind him.

'What dug?' Boaby asked looking around for any sign of a canine presence.

'He hasn't got a dog he's got a big torch but, maybe he will shine that on you' I said smiling to myself because Boaby didn't get it. Why would he.

We eventually got Searcher comfortable on the pavement across the other side of the street from the warehouse; the plan was to say he had fallen down the nearby stairs. As Ronnie started to let down the roller doors Boaby let out a yelp and ran towards him. I was tempted to shout at Boaby not to hit him but decided not to, if he wanted to hit him fair do's he could fill his boots for all I cared. But he ran right past Ronnie and into the warehouse, emerging a few minutes later, just as we could hear an approaching siren.

His arms were full of rectangular boxes and as he got nearer I asked 'What the fuck is that' and just as he answered with a huge grin Searcher and I answered with him 'Wine fucking gums'

I decided as I walked up Shields road with my box of wine gums that my days of crime were over. I mean real crime, not screwing the social for every penny I could get. I reluctantly decided that Charlie was right, the government in the shape of the she-witch thatcher had caused my unemployment, and since they had also made the so easily exploited rules then who was I to refuse to exploit them.

'I'm gonny tell the social that we have split up and that I am staying at my ma's' I told Patricia the next morning as she enjoyed her tea and toast and I enjoyed my breakfast of a bottle of *Strike Cola* and the remains of the wine gums.

'I don't want to fiddle the social Danny, you can get the jail for that' she said looking worried 'is it not just easier to get a job' I should have considered what she meant rather than the literal meaning of the words she spoke.

'No it isnae fuckin easier to get a job, I've been trying for months now and canny fuckin get anything. Do you seriously think I don't want to bloody work? Why are you saying that? Do you think I'm like all the lazy workshy bastards that hang about that minging bookies drinking *Super lager* all day?' I said throwing my cup of tea at the wall above her head. The cup shattered and the baby started howling. I felt sick to my stomach, thinking that part of the cup had hit him and maybe cut him. I dashed to the cot and lifted him, checking him for blood or scratches. But thankfully nothing had touched him; he had just been frightened by the unexpected noise of the cup exploding.

Patricia had been hit by a couple of pieces at the cup and had some tea spilled on her head, as the cup hadn't been empty. I would have felt better had she screamed and shouted at me, but she didn't she just looked at me with disgust as she got up from the bed and went to the mirror above the kitchen fireplace and started picking the shards of the cup out of her hair.

I put Patrick in his pram and threw a couple of nappies and his bottle in a carrier bag and took him for a walk, Patricia said nothing again. I wished she would stop saying nothing; it was getting on my nerves. At least if she said something I could argue it out with her, when she said nothing, that left me to argue it out with myself, and when I did that, I always lost.

Chapter Twenty Eight; Work at last.

It was becoming a repeating pattern. We got skint, Patricia got fed up being skint, and I got angry at Patricia being fed up, because in my head she was blaming me.

'Why can't you see it's not my fault, I can't get a job. Me and three million other poor fuckers can't get a job, it isnae just me' I screamed at the top of my voice. I was virtually incapable of talking in a reasonable tone any more. If I caught the merest whiff of criticism I exploded. Not only with Patricia with anyone and everyone. The owner of the bookies had told me to take a couple of weeks off because I had jumped down from where I was marking the board and head butted a guy for sarcastically asking if the social knew I was working in the bookies. He thought he was being funny, I disagreed.

The bookie didn't sack me he just told me to not come back for a couple of weeks until the fuss died down. Which I thought was good of him the customer I head butted didn't think so but as the bookie told him, he was an eejit and deserved all he got, the bookie offered to take a vote amongst his customers on who should be allowed back in the shop, me or the customer with the bloody nose and black eye, the customer declined the offer. Probably because of the laughter and shouts of the other customers questioning his education his diet and the legitimacy of his parentage, when they were calling him a stupid fat bastard.

‘I am trying to find something, you know I am so why start this shite again’ I screamed at Patricia again before the echoes of my first scream had even died out.

‘Danny, I never said you weren’t trying did I? I said I am fed up being skint, look at my shoes Danny’ she said lifting them up and showing me the soles. They had holes in the bottom that had been filled with pieces of black linoleum. I knew they had because it was me that had filled them. Patricia had been filling them with cardboard but I cleverly sussed out that linoleum would last longer. Before I could respond she shushed me.

‘And don’t scream that it isnae your fault, I’m not blaming you. I’m telling you that I’m fed up with it so I’m going back to work in the bingo. It’s not much it’s only a few shifts at the weekend but it’s better than nothing’

‘You canny do that’ I said.

‘You canny stop me’ she replied defiantly.

‘I mean they will stop your Monday book if you go back to work’ I explained, she only got the Monday book because she was claiming as a single unemployed parent. If she went back to work part time, we would be worse off financially ,in fact even if she went back to work full time we would be worse off.

‘Don’t be stupit how can me working full time make us worse off?’ she asked sceptically

‘Don’t ask me ask Maggie Thatcher’ I told her smugly.

‘Why would the woman who works in the chippy know anything?’ she asked.

It took me a few seconds to work out why this conversation was getting strange 'Naw the woman in the chip shop is Maggie Thompson, Maggie thatcher is the Prime Minister. She sets up all the rules for broo money'

'I don't think so, a woman widnae make it that you were better off no' working. And anyway you're always saying that Thatcher woman is an evil bitch that hates working class people. She canny hate them that much if she is making them better off by not working'

'You just don't understand politics, you canny go back to work at the bingo and that's that. Unless I get a job as well that is'

'Do you even want to work at the bingo? It's all women that work there except the manager and the caller and I think you might have to be a bit on the poofy side to be a caller.'

'Naw I don't want to work at the Bingo, I wisnae saying I want a job at the bingo. Just that unless both of us are working then it isnae worth you working or we lose money. If I'm working and you aren't we will be well off, and if I'm working and you want to then all that means is that you are working for nothing. And if I'm not working then you working will also mean you are working for nothing. Do you get it now?'

'Naw, my first shift is on Saturday afternoon starting at twelve, and then Sunday from twelve, so if you want to play football on Sunday morning then you need to take Patrick with you or get somebody to watch him.'

'You're not listening to me, if you go back to work then we lose money, you're not going back to work'

'Watch me' she said with finality.

She went back to work that Saturday. She had to hand in her Monday book and we became worst off by forty quid a week, she still refused to believe we could be worse off by her working even though we were worse off by her working. Luckily a few weeks later I landed a decent 'casual' job. I was back in the bookies doing all day Saturday for twenty five quid. One of the punters asked me a strange question. I had just given him some inside info about the dog track at Hackney, namely that when it was very wet huge puddles built up on the inside track and the high numbered dogs did much better than the low numbered dogs. He punted fairly heavily and thanks to my info that day won even more heavily.

'Do you know anything about nuts and bolts?' he asked as he counted his money from the last dog race at his now favourite track, I could see that this was a leading question so I played along and gave him the only answer a Glaswegian would give.

I told him 'I know everything about nuts and bolts, what I don't know about nuts and bolts isn't worth knowing. I have forgotten more about nuts and bolts than most people could learn in a lifetime'

'So not that much then' he correctly interpreted. He was also a Glaswegian.

'I know a wee bit actually, I did a bit of scaffolding and when I did my Scotvec engineering course I learned a little bit about different threads and materials' I answered a tad more honestly.

'Do you fancy a bit of part time work then?' He asked 'It should take you up to Christmas' he added.

'Abso-fuckin-lutely' I responded. 'How much?' I asked automatically.

'Fifteen quid a day, and all the nuts and bolts you can eat' he said.

'Five days a week?' I asked.

'Seven days a week if you want, but that might shorten the job, I have a couple of hundred pallets of nuts and bolts coming up from down south. My company bought them unseen, they want me to organise sorting them out and repackaging them for sale, do you fancy doing it for me?'

'Abso-fuckin-lutely' I responded and we shook hands on it.

I was very excited and couldn't wait to tell Patricia. It wasn't as simple as that, Charlie stopped his car at the door of the bookies just as I was walking through it.

'Get in the car' he shouted plainly in a hurry.

I got in the passenger seat and asked 'What's the hurry, who's chasing you or who are you chasing?

'Helen's been taking to hospital she is in labour' he said.

I waited for more detail, none came 'Helen who?' I asked.

'Dunky's Helen you dimwit she's having the wean'

'Okay fair enough but why are we in a hurry are they expecting us to deliver it or something? How bad is the NHS getting, it's pretty serious if they want us to be midwifes?

'Naw, shut up you bampot Dunky wants us to be there, he's in a bit of a panic and phoned me to get you and come down. Probably because he couldn'y get a hold of Donnie I suppose'

'Phoned you? Do you mean phoned your neighbour?' I asked.

'Naw he phoned me, I am on the phone now?' he grinned. He never could resist an opportunity to show off, not that I was bothered a phone seemed to be more hassle than it was worth as far as I could see. I remembered when my ma first got the phone in and our neighbours used to ask if they could use it all the time. My da put a wee wooden box with a slot in it beside the phone for them to put ten pence's in. Charlie learned immediately how to get the ten pence's out with a butter knife, I learned straight after him and so did Paul. It was always difficult for Paul to get away with it though. Whenever Charlie or I saw him at it we just waited patiently for him to finish emptying the box and then took the money from him. It wasn't as if he could run and stick us in to my da was it?

'He wants us there so why not? We were all there when Patricia had wee Patrick and you were there when Iris had wee Charlie.' He said shrugging his shoulders.

'Fair enough, but I haven't even met this lassie Helen yet, have you?

'Aye he brought her down the Old toll bar one Friday night, you and Patricia weren'y down that night. You were probably boracic'

'Tell me something new I'm always skint at the minute. What was she like, is she a nut-job the same as the last one. What's happening to her anyway is she still in Leverndale?' I asked

'She was the last time I heard, still delusional started saying her new man's a polis or something and he will sort out the McAllister's' he laughed.

'Don't laugh at her Charlie, that's not fair, I liked her before she went mental. She was alright sometimes, although we really should have known she was mentally suspicious when she agreed to marry Dunky. I think that's a reasonable definition of lunacy, actually agreeing to marry him I mean'

We got to the hospital a good six hours before Helen had the wean. We spent the six hours playing Chase the Lady, I won three quid off them at ten pence a game that shows how many games we played, and it probably wasn't fair to take Dunky's money he wasn't concentrating very well. Every time he heard a wean greet or a woman scream he jumped up and asked 'Is that it, is that me a daddy?'

Donnie arrived just before Helen dropped the wean. He turned up with a bottle of vodka and four plastic cups. 'To wet the weans head' he said.

As soon as we all swallowed our first half he said 'That's two quid each you owe me for the bottle'

Dunky was first to question his loyalty and memory 'When Annie had wee Mark, I took you on a pub crawl along tee Paisley Road and we both got absolutely steaming and not once did I ask you to put your haun in your pocket. What kind of miserable wee bastard are you?' which I thought was a fair question.

'A skint one' Donnie answered, looking for sympathy and understanding.

Charlie was next to question Donnie's memory 'When wee Maggie was born you came into the Viceroy and announced it to everybody, there were about ten of your pals there and you said to Peter behind the bar, get everybody a half on me, and then whispered to me to pay for it and you would square me up on Thursday when you got your wages. I'm still waiting'

'I don't remember that' was Donnie's predictable reply.

They turned to me to see how I would wriggle out of giving the miserable wee shite any money. I didn't I handed him two quid and said nothing. He looked at me and said 'If they two aren't paying its actually four quid you owe me' I tried in vain to get the two pound notes back out of his hand, but I'm pretty sure I would have needed a hacksaw and even then his fingers would probably still be shut tight holding on to the money.

We finished the vodka in less than twenty minutes, which meant I was half cut. But it made little or no difference to the other three. The midwife came out and asked 'Who's the father of Helen Stoddard's baby' three of us shrugged our shoulders and Donnie said 'him', pointing at Dunky.

'Oh aye it's me' Dunky said 'I forgot her name for a minute' he said flirtatiously to the midwife who must have been well over forty and glaikit looking.

She had a wee boy and Dunky was calling him David after my da, the place was getting filled up with David's, we had my da my ma wee brother and now my nephew it was bound to cause confusion at some point. Did nobody have any imagination in this family?

'Dunky and Donnie had plans to hit all the pubs on the Paisley Road again, Charlie said no he was driving but he would drop them off if they wanted. Apparently the bottle of vodka he had guzzled with us didn't affect his driving. I asked him if he could just drop me off at my house because I was skint. Dunky said no to worry about that he would carry me. It turned out to be five or six not one or two but I was alright by the time I walked home. I was still anxious to tell Patricia my good news

'You can pack your job in at the bingo' I said with the intent to surprise her with my news.

'We've been through this already. Naw' she responded 'in fact I'm sick of talking about it, I'm going to my ma's you can just watch Patrick' She picked up a bag that had been behind the couch.

'What's the bag for?' I asked angrily.

'I am going to stay with my ma for a few days, I'm fed up with you taking everything out on me and here you are steaming again. I'll give you ten minutes before you start screaming at me and accidentally bump me to the floor again' she said with some viciousness

'You canny just leave' I told her foolishly thinking I had a choice in this matter.

'There you go again, watch my lips YES I CAN' she shouted and stormed out slamming the door behind her.

I ran to the window and opened it and leapt out, I was at the mouth of the close before she got there.

‘I mean you canny because I am starting a new job on Monday, I’ve got a job’ I said beaming at her and no doubt bathing her in the delicious aroma of Tennants lager.

‘Well done whoopee for you’ she said and pushed past me. I must remember to tell her how sexy she is when she is angry and walking away in a temper, her bum jiggles about lovely so it does.

She came back the next day, I got the feeling that it was all an excuse for a night on the tiles, because I heard her and her pals at about two in the morning when I was up giving Patrick a bottle. They were singing *I don’t wanna dance,* I think they meant I really canny dance judging by the state of them. I held Patrick up kissed him on the top of his head and told him ‘That’s your drunken old mammy you can hear son’ he looked so proud.

Then they gave *Do you really want to hurt me* a go. One chancer popped his head out of his window and shouted ‘I will really want to hurt you if you don’t stop screeching under my windae’ I recognised the voice it was one of Patricia’s old boyfriends. That was a problem with me living in McCulloch Street; Patricia had lived here all her life so all of her old boyfriends lived here. So in the spirit of marking my territory, I popped my head out of the window and shouted at him ‘If you don’t want hurt you tadger then get your mouth and your windows shut’ that might mean a fight at the football the next day because we played for the same team, but who cares, I didn’t mind a fight at the football it got you warmed up for the game.

‘I love you Danny’ I am pretty sure it was Patricia that shouted but it was so slurred I couldn’t be sure.

‘I don’t’ was definitely shouted by her ex-boyfriend.

She came back the next morning. I told her all about the job and how we were going to be a £100 a week better off and since it was only eight weeks to Patricks first Christmas the timing couldn’t be better.

She made a list. Patricia loves lists. I hate lists. She sees a list as a plan, an ambition to aim towards. I see lists as a noose around my neck tightening as the days pass. Because she likes nothing better than making a list of unreasonable expectations and even puts a date on it for those expectations to be met. Bear in mind I hadn't even started this casual job yet. Bear in mind that the nature of casual work is day to day, I mean at any time the guy could say, cheers Danny but I don't need you anymore. This was her list to be completed by the end of 1982; she made it in the last week in October 1982.

A new house. Because Patrick was eight months now and needed his own room? A new suite (not just new to us but completely new from a furniture shop, not a second hand shop) because she was fed up with having a suite that had a board under the cushions to stop your arse hitting the floor, and anyway it was Darlene's old suite and that was reason enough. A new cooker because only one ring and one side of the oven worked; which was fair enough because I was sick of eating pies that were burnt on one side and still freezing on the other. Every time I said to her 'Why don't you turn the pies round half way through cooking?' she would say 'oh aye, so I should' but she never did.

New clothes and shoes for her because she claimed that her wedding dress was wearing out now that she had been wearing it every day for nearly two years. (Very funny) I disputed her need for new shoes telling her that since I had put lino in the soles of her shoes they were like brand new now. She disputed how funny that was. When I asked why there were no clothes or shoes on her list for me, she told me that as I had always been a tramp that my own family wouldn't recognise me if I turned up in new clothes. Which I agreed was a fair point. She suggested I should ask Donnie and Dunky if they had grown out of any of their stuff since that was my usual route for clothes and shoes. Very funny. I was now at least six inches taller than Donnie, and Dunky dressed like a homosexual clown. It was the eighties and he still thought he was a pimp from Starsky and Hutch.

There were also a few things on her list for Patrick which I didn't object to, although she objected to me wanting to buy him *Scaletrix* and a full size pool table. She claimed since he would only be nine months at Christmas that they weren't really for him. My explanation that he would grow into them fell on deaf ears.

After a couple of days I found her list in the back of her purse and binned it. She laughed in my face when she showed me the copy she had made because she knew I would find the first one and bin it. She claimed to have made six copies which probably meant she had made ten. I would never find them all.

Item one on her list mysteriously happened almost overnight, we got a letter from *The West of Scotland Housing Association* who were our landlords. The house we were in was actually half a house, the other half had been occupied by Charlie and Iris and then Patricia's ma. The landlord was apparently short of three and four bedroom houses and wanted to reinstate those two houses into one, and was willing to give us a two bedroomed house at 115 McCulloch Street if we wanted it. We immediately agreed and moved into the new house within three days. The landlord didn't think it through though because Patricia's ma said no she was happy where she was and wasn't moving. Her explanation was that she had previously lived in a haunted house for more than ten years. This house wasn't haunted so she wasn't prepared to risk moving into another house which might be haunted.

I also think that Patricia's brother didn't want to move because he had recently went to a lot of bother painting his bedroom jet black and building a scaffolding bed frame and furniture in it. We didn't care as we got a bigger house, it was one flight up with no garden, but since the only thing we had in the tiny strip of concrete that was supposed to be a garden in our last house was a broken pram and empty flower pots we decided that we could live without rolling lawns and flowerbeds for the moment.

Although the new house had two bedrooms and a larger bathroom, the living room and kitchen were one room. We didn't actually mind that, it meant you could be cooking the dinner or making a cup of tea and not miss what was on the telly.

I built a partition, a breakfast bar sort of thing to separate the kitchen from the living room it was about chest height with a black *Contiboard* shelf at the top. I did the back front and sides in brick effect wallboard. Patricia liked it, I was very proud, it was probably the first thing I had done in our house that she liked. I then got a football team mate of mine, who was a brickies, to come and build a real brick fireplace the whole length of the wall in the living room. With shelves at different heights to hold ornaments and lamps and what not. Patricia loved it, maybe I going up in her estimation and maybe not.

We also got a new suite and cooker, we couldn't afford to buy them so we got them on the never, from one of Patricia's pals' catalogue. The suite was an ultra-modern corner unit, Patricia still has a photograph of it she loved it so much.

So everything was looking good for Patricks first Christmas, we could afford everything we wanted for him and Patricia got new shoes and a new outfit for the New Year party at my ma's, which we were both looking forward to. Dorothy and Darlene were both coming through from England. Apparently Darlene was thinking about moving to Redcar to be nearer Dot. The between the lines message was that she was still having a hard time with big John. My ma was worried because at least if they were in Glasgow or at the worst Redcar somebody could keep an eye on her and him, a black eye or two wasn't unknown and that was just on him.

The short term casual work was becoming more solid. There was so much stuff coming up from Birmingham that Donnie McNair the guy who offered me the work had took three other people on and asked me to supervise them. He had also asked me to go full time on the books when we came back after the New Year, I asked him if I could think about it because going full time would lose me £60 a week, which was a lot of money. He agreed we would talk about it mid-January but he would prefer me to be on the books.

He was one of the good guys, I made sure I got him a nice bottle of scotch for his Ne'erday and I also handed in a nice wee Christmas present for his daughter Lynne she was only about four or five but you could tell already wee Lynne McNair would be breaking hearts when she was older and wiser.

Patricia's list was actually complete seven days before Christmas, she missed out one item on her wish list though; a get out of jail free card for me.

It wasn't my fault I got the jail three days before Christmas it was Charlie's, of course. Four nights before Christmas we were down in the Quaich playing darts. I was flush because I had just had a wee Christmas bonus win on the dogs of £80 which was all mines as I had conveniently forgotten to mention it to Patricia. I slipped Dunky twenty quid because he was always slipping me money and he was out of work at the time. I bought the first three or four rounds for Charlie and Donnie because Charlie also slipped plenty of cash my way when he was flush and Donnie, well Donnie was my brother and I'm sure he must have slipped me something sometime, I just can't remember it.

'Are you doing anything tomorrow?' Charlie asked me.

I reacted in the correct and proper way when Charlie asked you a question; with suspicion. 'Why?' I said, aware that I had had too much to drink to properly deal with Charlie if he was up to something.

He grinned his shark like grin and said 'I need a wee favour, I've got a bit of business with a guy in the snooker hall at St George's Cross, and I could do with somebody watching my back'

'Does watching your back involve shooting anybody' I asked.

He laughed 'Naw'

'Stabbing anybody' I asked.

He laughed again 'Naw'

'Fighting with anybody then?'

He laughed for the third time 'What is it you take me for? Probably not'

'Probably not means definitely aye, it's only a few days to Christmas Charlie just leave whatever it is to after the new year and I'll come along then' I offered. 'And anyway, what's up with Searcher and big Boaby can they no' help you out'

'It's Searcher and big Boaby I am going to meet' he said with a grimace.

'No way Charlie, they are your best pals, their still my best pals as well even if I don't see them that much. What the hell have you done to them' I asked.

'Why do you think it's me that's done something to them and no' them that's done something to me?'

I smiled at him, he smiled back. 'Fair enough, Searcher thinks I done him out of some cash. He gave me some gear to move on for him and told me what he wanted for it, I added a wee bit on top and he got upset. I think he was upset because I made more money out of the job than him' he grinned again full of himself.

'Did he get anything at all?' I asked.

'You really do have a low opinion of me' he said and added 'Not much really'

I agreed that he should pick me up and I would go with him, I was more intent on being a peace-maker than helping him fight with our friends. Patricia was told we were going to play golf; Charlie had recently taken up playing at the public course in Ruchhill where my Da and his two brothers played occasionally. Donnie and Dunky also joined them from time to time, so it was a reasonable expectation that I would become involved at some point.

Charlie turned up at one o'clock the next afternoon full of his usual smiling enthusiasm.

'This isnae good Charlie, fighting with searcher and big Boaby, their on our side, and by the way what's that awful smell in here, it smells like gas' I said as soon as I got in his car.

'Somebody threw one of them smoke canisters you get at the football and it landed in my car' he said sheepishly.

'Who the hell did that? What a dickhead.'

He laughed out loud 'It was me'

I said nothing and waited for the tale of his latest stupidity, I didn't wait long.

'I bought ten boxes of smoke canisters for next to nothing I was going to sell them the next time I was down at Parkhead or Ibrox, but they are French or Polish or something so I wanted to see what colour they were and if they were any good. So I went along to the back end of Glasgow Green last night to try one' He stopped just to have a right good laugh. 'It was so funny Danny you would have pished yourself. To cut a short story shorter, I pulled the wee tab to start the smoke with the intention of lobbing the canister as far as I could. But as soon as I pulled the tab the bastard thing heated up where I was holding it and burnt my hand' He again paused to show me a tiny red patch on his hand, it was hardly noticeable at all.

'So I panicked a wee bit and dropped the canister but before it hit the ground I swung my boot at it, thinking I could kick it away. But it was heavy and all I did was kick it in through the window of the car and within ten seconds there was purple smoke vomiting out of the car in all directions' he finished with another hearty laugh.

'Purple smoke? What football team in Scotland plays in purple? In fact what football team anywhere plays in purple?' I asked more interested in looking for a way to recover his money than his stupidity.

'Aberdeen' he answered emphatically.

'Aberdeen play in red you fanny' was my considered response.

'I know' he said with a grin 'but they sheep shagging bastards will buy anything if it's cheap enough and anyway they can call it a tribute to Alex Fergusons nose'

'Aye okay that will work' I answered and we went towards our date with Searcher with a smile on our faces. Charlie's grin widened when *Soft Cell's Tainted Love* came on the radio, for some bizarre reason him and Iris absolutely loved that song. He decided the song would be even better if he sang along, he was wrong.

The snooker hall was at the bottom of Maryhill road and it was one we visited quite frequently, we were all avid snooker and pool players some of us better than others. I was the worst, but could usually beat Dunky in a long match he would win the first two or three frames and I would win the rest because he was drunk.

'Hi Willie, how's it gaun' Charlie said as we entered the dark cold hall. It was lit with very low wattage bulbs except for the canopies above the tables which threw brilliant white light onto the green baize. So when you were within a couple of feet of the tables it was light but outside the perimeter of the tables it was dark and gloomy, full of shadows.

'Ahm aw right Charlie, what about yourself pal, are you getting a turn?' Willie Hepburn responded. Willie was an okay sort of guy; we rented the tables by the hour. We would normally pay for a two hour rental and get four hours, slipping Willie a couple of quid on the way out. As I said he was one of the good guys and knew when to turn a blind eye. The same couldn't be said for his wee boy, William, he was about fifteen and seemed to be there all the time. He was a stocky wee bugger with a crew cut; NHS round spectacles and a nose that always had snotters hanging from it. He would wander in and out of the table's earywigging and sticking his neb in where it wasn't appreciated. More than once one of us had to put our boot up his arse to get rid of him. Because he was there all the time he was a very good snooker player and his favourite trick was to hustle strangers. So he would loiter about between tables trying to find an eejit to skin.

'I've a wee bit of business today, so keep away from my table young Willie' Charlie told him when he spotted him loitering behind his dad.

'It's William' the wee man retorted with venom, we all knew he didn't like being called Willie, which is why nobody ever called him anything else. But at least he heeded the warning and stayed out of sight.

Charlie and I had a quick game of snooker before Searcher arrived, he gave me 21 of a start and beat me before we got to the colours, I would have to renegotiate my handicap.

'Charlie how you doing, you got my cash?' searcher said as soon as he entered the pool of light surrounding our table. Boaby was just at his back in the shadows.

I took a tighter grip on my snooker cue, actually it was a club cue, and I hadn't brought mine with me, because we were there to fight not to play snooker. Come to think of it maybe that's why Charlie beat me; I had been using a rubbish cue.

Charlie burst out laughing 'you're not the full shilling Searcher I mean it, what way is that to say hello to your bestest pals. Grab a cue; we can have a wee game of doubles. Me and Danny will play you and Boaby for the money'

Searcher smiled but the smile didn't reach his eyes 'so you admit that you owe me money Charlie, you admit that you have ripped off one of your *bestest pals* then?' he asked sardonically.

'Look wee man you wanted some gear shifting, I offered you a price and I moved the gear on for a better price. I don't think that's ripping you off, that's just business *hopalong*' Charlie said, deliberately baiting Searcher. Searcher just smiled his cold grin but I couldn't avoid butting in. I still blamed myself for Searcher getting knocked down and injuring his leg permanently.

'You can stop that pish Charlie, Searcher is our mate and Boaby's liable to rip you a new arsehole with his teeth if you keep that going' I said angrily, I don't mind backing him up and if it comes to it I will take a kicking for him if necessary but I wasn't going to let him start a fight for nothing, not while we were sober anyway.

'How much money are we talking about anyway?' I asked, as if either of them would give me an honest answer.

'He owes me a hundred quid' Searcher said wisely ignoring Charlie's attempts to wind him up.

'Are you fucking kidding Search' Boaby butted in this time 'A hundred quid, you're gonny fall out with Charlie and Danny for a hundred quid? I'll give you the hundred quid and we can settle down and have a game of snooker and get rat arsed'

I laughed and said 'Right that's it settled, who wants a pint'

'I don't want any money from Boaby; I don't even really want any money from Charlie. I want him to apologise for ripping me off' searcher said his cold sly little grin back on his face. It was clear to me that both of them, Searcher and Charlie, wanted to keep this going. It was clearly a pride thing and I'm a McCallister, the biggest part of any trouble I ever get into is because of misplaced pride. Whether it's an argument with Patricia, or family, or friends, or even strangers, pride is usually at the bottom of it. And Charlie was worse for it than me.

'Okay' he said 'you want an apology. I'm sorry that you are a stupid wee bastard that didn't know the worth of what he was trying to sell. And I'm sorry that I need to kick your head in because you don't understand that you are a stupid wee crippled bastard'

It could have went two ways at that point, my original plan had been to lay into big Boaby as soon as the fists started flying, my reasoning being that I had to hit him with the snooker cue at least ten times to make it a fair fight, otherwise he would knock me out with one punch. Fortunately Boaby was of the same mind as me, if we needed to fight each other then so be it. But this was just nonsense between two half-wits and there was no need to let it go too far.

Boaby grabbed Searcher and I got in front of Charlie, they managed to throw a few punches each before we stopped them in their tracks and, and as usual Charlie got a sneaky one in. I hadn't quite got a firm grip of him but Boaby had Searcher well wrapped up when Charlie snaked his arm around me and gave searcher a hard dig to the ribs. As expected Searcher came off worse he had blood pouring from his nose and a red mark round his eye which would be a shiner by later that day, he was also obviously in pain from the dirty late blow from Charlie. The only significant blow Searcher had landed on Charlie was a punch to his kidneys which Charlie was doing his best to give the impression that it hadn't hurt him. I knew different he felt it alright.

Both of them stood there huffing and puffing after their little dance and still eyeing each other warily. Charlie held his hand out and Searcher looked at it and pondered it briefly but he shook it eventually and smiled his real smile and said 'That's it settled then as long as you know that if you ever rip me off again then I won't let it go as easy'

'Fair enough' Charlie said 'But you need to promise to stop being a stupid wee bastard' that hung in the air for a second before Searcher accepted it for the joke that it was. Problem solved, I thought, time for a few games of snooker, if Searcher would take the bait and have Boaby on his side versus me and Charlie we might even take a few quid off them.

'What kind of wee lassie's fight was that for fuck sake?'

This came from behind us from the gloom between the tables, the big mouth that said it emerged and before I could blink Charlie grabbed the snooker cue out of my hands and started swinging it with good effect at the owner of the voice. Mayhem then followed there were snooker balls and cues being sprayed about the room with quite a few hitting their intended targets, a blue ball hit me on the stomach just above the crown jewels. As it dropped to the floor, Charlie, despite being otherwise engaged in holding a guy on a snooker table by his throat and punching his lights out still managed to ask me 'Is that one of yours on the floor or is it a snooker ball'

I was for once too preoccupied to think up a witty return, I had two guys taking turns at trying to kick me as I scrambled about on the floor trying to get away from them or at least avoid being kicked. Boaby head butted one of them and to my surprise the other one was grabbed in an arm-lock by a policeman. Behind that policeman there were another six policemen. So I wasn't all that surprised to be grabbed by the hair and handcuffed to a snooker table with the added benefit of a severe kick in the ribs from one of Glasgow's finest.

Three days before wee Patrick's first Christmas and I was lying in a police cell somewhere in Maryhill, Patricia was going to go bananas. We were just getting things on track, I was working and claiming the dole, and she was working and still had a Monday book which all meant that we had a wee bit of spare cash to do the house up. There was a fair chance I could be remanded for this, one or two of our opponents were in quite a bad way, the kind of bad way you get into when boaby head butts you to sleep or Charlie plays your head like a bongo drum. If I did get remanded it would mean Christmas and New Year in Barlinnie. I had been remanded overnight in Barlinnie once; I had no desire whatsoever to repeat the experience.

Luckily for me and the rest of us, wee William Hepburn and his dad both told the police that the guys we had set about had come straight into the snooker hall and attacked us with no provocation on our part at all. Maybe I had the wee man wrong maybe he wisnae just a snottery wee big headed shite after all. But the very next time I saw him was in the same snooker hall and he was back to his old tricks of hovering about in the shadows earywigging and trying to hustle people, so I was right the first time he was just a horrible wee shite.

It turned out that Charlie had been fighting with the boy with the big mouth the last time he had been in the snooker hall. The guy obviously fancied his chances of revenge since he was four of his mates and in his head five against four seemed like good odds. I can only imagine he never saw Boaby standing there. The police let us out that night, so fortunately that meant I never had to explain myself to Patricia. But I had had enough it did strengthen my resolve to absolutely stop letting Charlie get me into bother, I was trying to be a grown up. But then again I could have said no I'm not coming with you couldn't I? It also made me think of something my da used to ask me 'If Charlie threw himself in the Clyde, would you do it as well?' unfortunately for me the answer was yes and in fact I did exactly that about ten years later.

My problem was that when Charlie threw himself in the Clyde metaphorically he normally emerged with a salmon in his mouth, when I followed him in metaphorically I came out covered in shite. So that was it, no more getting into bother because of Charlie.

Christmas in 1982 was superb, we got up early and opened all of our presents, we gave Patrick a hand to open his because he was still only nine months old. We were more enthusiastic about his presents than he was, but there was a heavy duty rattle that he particularly liked, what he liked most about it was the sound it made when it hit my head, strangely enough Patricia liked that sound as much as he did. We had a quick roll and square slice for our breakfast and headed down to my Ma's for Christmas dinner.

Dorothy was through from Redcar for Christmas and Darlene was there as well, it was her intention after the New Year to move to Redcar in fact she had already managed to get a council house in South Bank, not the prettiest of housing schemes apparently but not the worst either. Dunky was coming along with his new girlfriend Helen and their wee boy David even though he was only weeks old, Patricia thought the wean was too young to be taken to a Christmas party but it was their wean, their choice.

Charlie and iris were spending it with her ma and da but promised to come down at the New Year before Darlene and Dot went home to Redcar.

Donnie and Annie might or might not turn up after Christmas dinner for a wee while; because as big as my ma's living room was, there was no way we could all sit round the makeshift table. Some of us had offered to sit on the couch and armchairs but my ma wasn't having that. We also suggested bringing the kitchen table into the living room. But my ma needed that for preparing and serving the dinner. So Donnie and Annie decided to have their Christmas dinner in Pollok and then, if they felt like it take a walk down to my ma's with the weans afterwards.

It turned out that they did and my ma's house was full to the rafters with screaming weans. Not just that but David, (my youngest brother, not my da or my nephew) Donnie's oldest boy mark and dot's oldest boy wee Tony all got drunk on cider and babysham. It was completely hilarious. David was so drunk he peed his trousers, he made it to the toilet but couldn't get his wee man out in time, although to be fair it was kind of difficult to find even when sober. I took him ben the room to get him changed before my ma saw him. In the room were wee Tony and Mark singing and dancing to that year's Christmas number one. *Save your love by Renee and Renatta.*

I don't think Mark and wee Tony were ever going to make it big in the music industry, especially since wee Tony was having terrible problems with his hearing at the time. This meant that nearly anything you said he would say 'What?' and you had to keep repeating yourself. It also made him tend to shout, which wasn't great when he was singing. Mark showed his appreciation of Tony's shouting of *save your love my darling, save your love*, in a rubbish Italian accent by bending over and vomiting between his feet. It might not have been so bad had he not splashed his vomit all over my new shoes and trousers.

I only pushed him back to stop him vomiting all over me again. But as he staggered back under the force of my push he tripped over David's legs. David had just rolled off the edge of the bed because the eejit had been trying to lie down on the bed and change his underpants under a towel which he had spread across his naughty bits. He was twelve years old at the time maybe he was trying to hide his first pube or something.

Mark tripped over his legs anyway and fell and whacked his head on the edge of the set of drawers beside the bed. Mark must have a soft head because this pathetic wee bump split it open. And all of a sudden there is blood running down his face and mingling with the vomit on his tee shirt. I wiped the vomit of my trouser legs using David's clean underpants he had been unable to get on. I then told them they were on their own and left the room. I did go back in a wee while later to make sure none of them were dead. Tony was still singing in an Italian accent but this time he was murdering *Eye of the tiger.* One of them must have seen to Mark's cut because he had a full strip of *Elastoplast* stuck to his hair and David had given up trying to get dressed. He was lying flat out on the floor proving me wrong, he didn't have any pubes yet.

Dunky got drunk, what a shocker eh? Helen his new girlfriend went back to their house in a taxi and left him sleeping on the armchair next to the fire. She said that he had got drunk so quick because they were both suffering from a lack of sleep. So she would just leave him there and he could go home in the morning. Twenty minutes after she left he got his second wind and was up dancing with Darlene to Elvis Presley songs that Paul had put on when nobody was looking.

It wasn't all the drink and stupidity that made Christmas 1982 brilliant. It was half an hour or so that me and Patricia spent in the kitchen with my ma at about three in the morning.

'Who's got Patrick' my ma asked us.

Patricia answered 'My ma's got him in our house; she was having a quiet Ne'erday anyway and didnae mind watching him'

'That's good' my ma said 'are youse two alright, are youse happy?'

We both said 'Aye' at the same time. 'We sometimes argue when we have no money' Patricia added.

'Everybody does sweetheart, but it's daft you know. Money is the least important thing in the world. What matters is that you are healthy and happy and that your wean is healthy and happy. Money always turns up, you will'ny starve. It isnae Africa.' She said.

'Has he lifted his hauns to you yet hen?' my ma asked Patricia as if I wasn't there.

Patricia hesitated before replying 'Naw no yet' She was thinking about the time I pushed her or at least she thought I pushed her. My ma ignored her hesitation and said 'The first time he does, jail him'

Patricia and I were both slightly taken aback by this and looked at each other, my ma caught the glance.

'Things are changing hen, and it's about bloody time. The polis would never do anything when a man slapped his wife when I was first married. Why would they, that's the way it was. That's the way men shaped their women how they wanted them. But not now darling, trust me the polis are starting to listen to women. They might not do anything about a wee slap now and again but if he lifts his fists, they will jail him'

'Hold on a minute ma, I've never lifted a finger to Patricia and I never would' maybe my ma spotted the guilty glance I had at Patricia and Patricia putting her head down in response.

'You will' she said with certainty 'You're your da's son, youse all are. Youse all think you can take on the world and solve all your problems with your fists. Well you canny Danny' and she giggled.

'You canny Danny, that's a wee poem' she said 'Danny son, you're supposed to be the brainbox in the family. Try and rise above it will you, for your sake as well as hers.' she said smiling at me. That smile told me she doubted if I could be different and maybe she was right. Maybe I couldn't, maybe I would be the same as all the rest.

We could hear somebody in the living room shouting 'Turn that music off and give us a song Davie' they were talking to my da and he didn't need to be asked twice. He sang *Mack the knife* and as usual brought the house down. My ma sung the words along with him but not loud enough for anybody except us to hear. When my da was finished and the rest of them were trying to decide who was next to sing, my ma started softly singing in the kitchen. *Moon River* and it was beautiful, I had heard her sing it hundreds of times. But usually at parties when people were talking and glasses were clinking or other people joined in the chorus. This time it was just her, her sweet sweet voice and me with the woman I loved. I can hear her still; I only need to close my eyes. She spent the next twenty minutes or so reminiscing about when she was young before she met my da. I could see the fourteen year old girl she had been in her twinkling eyes, she never talked much about herself so when she did I listened and enjoyed.

We stayed the night sleeping on the couch, which we were lucky to get the house was completely full. Not so much lucky as smart, as it started to get late I pulled Patricia onto the couch beside me and each time somebody stood up we stretched out a bit further until eventually we were occupying the whole thing. In the morning me and Dunky made everybody something to eat, he made the rolls and bacon or rolls and egg and I made all the weans French toast.

Although the three drunken and hung-over twelve year olds might have objected to me calling them weans.

Patricia and I walked up Shields road, it was cold but we weren't bothered we were happy with each other and frequently stopped for a wee winch and a cuddle to heat each other up. In fact once or twice we almost got too heated up. I almost convinced her that some al fresco loving was in order until she noticed we were standing under a sign that said Milnpark Street pumping station. She wasn't amused and reckoned I was trying to seduce her so I could point out the sign and make a joke about it later. Everything was perfect so how come within a few hours we were fighting like a cat and dog.

Chapter twenty nine; and then there were four.

'I've had enough I'm going to my ma's'

This was becoming almost a weekly thing with Patricia over one thing or another and every time I was getting the better of the argument she would throw some stuff in a carrier bag and go to her ma's house. I suspect it was for a bit of peace and quiet really, but it was starting to get on my wick. Patrick wasn't exactly keeping regular hours, his favourite trick at the time, (he was about nine months old) was to wake up at four in the morning and scream blue murder for a bottle and then refuse to go back to sleep. Most of the time I was happy to indulge him, there's nothing like getting the wee barra giggling in the middle of the night. He had a right hearty wee laugh which was very infectious, I left for work at half six so it wasn't that big a deal for me.

But Patricia was taking more midweek shifts at the bingo which meant she didn't get in till after eleven at night. By the time she had a bath or a shower and something to eat it was one or two o'clock in the morning before she got to bed. I don't suppose she found the wee man laughing at four o'clock in the morning as much fun as I did. The worst of it was that she would shout and bawl at me in the middle of the night. Telling me that it was because I was playing with him that he was laughing as much, if I would just keep quiet when I was feeding him he would go back to sleep she reckoned.

I told her she was talking crap it was Patrick that was keeping me up. I would lie there giving him his bottle and when he started to look drowsy I would pretend to shut my eyes so that he would copy me and fall into a sleep. But he didn't, when I shut my eyes he poked his finger in one of them or grabbed my nose with his sharp wee nails and scratched it. And as soon as I said 'Ouch' the wee jobby would start his giggling and then I would laugh and that would make him worse and he would laugh harder and that would just make me worse and my laughing would wake her up. It was terrible at times. I think he had a wee nasty streak, if I had a weak spot he would find it, if I had a scab he would pick at it. He wasn't even a year old so how come he was able to hold his sick in until I lifted him above my head and then let it go all over my face and sometimes in my mouth. Or how come he liked nothing better than to pee in my face as soon as I opened his nappy to change it. Patricia said it was coincidence, aye right, so it was.

This wasn't the best time for her to piss off to her ma's for a sleep. It was Boxing day, but I was due in to work the next day, the firm I worked for, P&W McClellan' always did their stock take between Christmas and New Year and paid a forty quid bonus on top of your wages for the three days, to everybody who came in and helped with the stock take. They also laid on fish suppers at dinner time and bacon rolls and soup in the mornings. This was my first year with them but the other guys let me know that not turning up for stocktake left your coat on a shaky hook. And since I was only working there on the casual it would most probably leave me back on the broo (not that I had signed off yet).

So there was nothing else for it, if she insisted on staying in her ma's then Patrick was going with her, which would put her gas at a peep. If she was only going along there to get away from his through-the-night shenanigans then there wasn't much point in her going if I insisted she took him with her.

I put Patrick in his buggy wrapped a blanket around him and walked him along the street to his grannies house it was past his bed time and he was getting ratty, I lifted Patrick and the buggy up the three steps into her ma's close and as soon as I went into the close I could hear shouting, it was Patricia shouting at her brother Rob.

'Don't be such a stupid wee liar and tell my ma the truth' she screamed at him as she pushed him about in the loaby of her ma's house.

'Gonny stop screaming, you'se are frightening the wean' I said as I went into her ma's house.

Her ma joined me in telling them both to settle down and stop the shouting. I put the wee man through in her ma's bedroom and sat with him for a minute or two, as soon as he had his dummy tit in his mouth he started slurping away at it and was sleeping in five minutes. He was funny with the dummy, if you tried to pull it out he would suck as hard as he could to hang on to it and when you tried to put it back in he was like a wee hoover moving his face from side to side and trying to suck it in. When I went into the kitchen Patricia and Rob were still at it.

'Robert, tell my ma the bloody truth you're really getting on my nerves with this now' Patricia said. Her ma told her to shut up, again. I had never seen Patricia get this angry unless it was with me.

'What's the Hampden' I said trying to lighten the mood.

'The what?' her ma asked.

'The Hampden roar, the score. It means what's going on' I explained patiently.

'This eejit has been eating stuff out of my ma's Christmas hamper and telling her that I have been coming into her house when she's out and stealing it for us' Patricia said to me, absolutely fuming so she was.

'You have been taking it, I never said stealing it' Rob said petulantly, he had only just turned fifteen and was as annoying as only a teenager can be.

Patricia pushed him and could only utter a sound like uggh she was so angry now that she could hardly talk 'what is the difference between stealing and taking something that isnae yours you idiot' she shouted at him and pushed him again. I wasn't getting the reason for her to be so very angry; it was no big deal, an argument over nonsense as far as I could see.

'What is that's missing Jean and I will replace it tomorrow when the shops open' I said trying to calm everyone down and bring the argy bargy to an end.

'It was a tin of boiled ham and ….' Jean started to say but was interrupted by Patricia shouting at me now.

'Naw you won't I never took anything, so you're no replacing anything' she shouted at me and then turned to Rob. 'Tell my ma why you're eating all the stuff out the hamper, tell her' she screamed in his face. 'I've had to put up with your shit for years, you never do anything wrong according to her do you? Well no' this time tell her the truth before I tell her'

'I am telling her the truth; you took it because you and him are always skint and you're always taking grub out of her press' Rob said head down looking at his feet.

Patricia went to hit him but I stood between them. 'Naw we never touched a thing you wee prick, it was you with the munchies that's what the problem is' she said softly.

I laughed out loud, Jean looked perplexed 'What the hell's the munchies?' she asked. I laughed again. But Patricia filled her in.

'When you sit smoking hash all day and all night sometimes it makes you really hungry and that's called the munchies and when you get them you will eat absolutely anything' she said with relish and stared vindictively at Rob, daring him to deny it..

'You're just saying that to cover up you stealing Danny's money' Rob said. My grin was still there but reducing in intensity. 'She takes your money to get something for your tea and then comes in here and takes something out of the press and keeps the money'

'She canny steals from me Rob, my money is her money. It's a decent enough try at trying to change the subject Rob, but there's something you should know about your sister son. She doesn't go to the shops for food wee man, I do. We do the shopping on a Saturday morning up at the Fine Fare on Pollokshaws Road and when we need anything during the week I go to the shop no' her. She will even take her tea black rather than move her arse along to the end of the street and get milk. So grow up dickhead and tell your ma about you doing drugs and scoffing all her hamper when you get the munchies' I said starting to get angry.

He wouldn't or couldn't stop, he was a teenager, a morose spoiled brat of a teenager, there was about as much chance of him stopping lying as me giving up drinking.

'You think she's miss nice and innocent' he shouted at me 'she comes up here every week drinking with her pals and laughs at you being stuck in with your wean and tells her pals that she makes up daft arguments to get out of the house and drink with them all the time' he shouted pointing his finger in my face and spraying me with saliva as he shouted, he was too close.

He was far too close and I did something incredibly stupid, I head butted him. It was absolutely unnecessary and I instantly regretted it but he was so close to me that I think I just did it instinctively.

When somebody gets that close that's what I do on the positive side as head butts go this one was ten out of ten. It landed squarely on his nose which burst with a spray of blood like a geyser. He was standing with his back to the kitchen door when I hit him which had the unfortunate effect that he bounced back off it towards me. Which with me being an idiot made me think he was fighting back so I moved to the side and moved as if to punch him? Luckily for me, and him, Patricia jumped between us to break it up.

Jean went mental and no wonder I was twenty one and had just about knocked her fifteen year old boy into next week. She laid into me, slapping me and kicking my legs and the punched into my back as she began pushing me out the kitchen door along the hall and out the front door. Telling me what she thought of me in swear words that would have made a docker blush. Patricia followed me out and we walked a few yards towards our own house when I stopped and turned back.

'Just leave it Danny, he's only fifteen, you shouldn't have hit him and you're no' going back to do it again. I won't let you' she said.

'I need to go back' I said with a dark scowl on my face.

'Naw you don't' she said grabbing my arm and dragging me away.

I grinned at her extracted my arm from her grip and said 'I do need to go back; we have left Patrick in your ma's bedroom'

She did smile a tiny wee bit but maybe she wasn't particularly in the mood for my games. 'I'll get him, you go along to the house, I won't be long. If you go in there it will just make my ma worse'

'Are you coming home later?' I asked 'You're no just going in there to have a drink and give your pal's a shout are you?' I grinned at her. She just shook her head and looked angry, what had I said wrong now?

'You believed that idiot don't you' she said with a look of disappointment on her face.

'Naw I didn'y' I said 'giving her a wee cuddle, but I think I did kind of believe what David had said, no smoke without fire, I thought.

I worked the next few days and managed to avoid Patricia's ma and I even managed to avoid annoying Patricia for four days in a row, which was a world record. I saw Rob in the street and tried to apologise to him, especially when I saw the shape of his nose and the black eye which was the result of me head butting him. I was actually proud of that head butt but obviously not that it was him that I headered, it was just the perfect execution of the blow that I was proud of. It seemed didn't share my joy at my expertise.

Hogmanay and the New Year were pretty good that year as well. First of all Patricia's ma was staying in and going to bed early she was skint and couldn't be bothered with the New Year. I suggested to Patricia we slip her a fiver for a half bottle of Bells whisky so she could have a wee drink. Patricia agreed but told me to give her the fiver the following day.

'That won't get her a drink at midnight' I said.

'I know, but it means that she can watch Patrick for us, and the fiver will get her some messages in tomorrow instead of being wasted on drink' Patricia said with a sneaky smile on her face.

'You can be really thoughtful and kind sometimes' I said, I am sure she noticed the sarcasm but she just nodded 'I know' and grinned again.

Darlene was already half drunk when we got to my ma's and it was only eleven o'clock at night. Normally my ma didn't allow drinking before the bells so Darlene must have got drunk and came in like that.

'Why are you half puggled already' I asked her as soon as she walked in to the kitchen.

'Who are you? The drinking polis?' she asked me immediately getting on her high horse ready to fight, the fact that I had a go at her first was lost on me.

'You know my ma likes nobody to drink until after the bells so why are you drunk and where's your useless shitebag of a man?' I said back always ready to argue with Darlene when the chance presented itself.

'He's at his ma's and I would like to see you calling him a shitebag when he comes in. But you won't, you say one thing behind his back and another behind his face you hypochondriac' she slurred 'and where's Barbie?' she retorted aiming her barb at Patricia who did actually have long blonde hair, and come to think of it she was just as nicely proportioned as Barbie, except maybe a wee bit more top heavy but who's complaining?

I smiled it was a decent enough dig from Darlene 'No idea, maybe she's in the living room looking for Ken' I said which got a snigger from Charlie who had just arrived with a party sized carry out. He had 24 cans of Tennent's lager and at least three bottles of spirits in a Haddows bag. He put it all down and then took a wee miniature bottle of Babysham out of his inside pocket. 'For Iris' he announced with a huge grin implying the rest of the booze was for him.

'Seems like a fair swap' I said without thinking.

'What does that mean' he asked with fury in his eyes.

'It's a joke' I said quickly 'Calm down, it's only a wee joke'

Darlene butted in 'You've been here five minutes and you've argued with me and Charlie already.'

'I'm no' arguing with Charlie or you, all I asked you was why you were half drunk before the bells.' I said to her trying to calm the situation down before it got out of hand.

'How who are you, the drinking polis' Charlie asked me with his big grin, he had clearly heard the beginning of my conversation with Darlene. 'And your man is a shitebag Darlene, he might be at his ma's but he won't come up here tonight. He knows that we know about your wee black eye problems a couple of months ago. Dot told my ma and she told us so he won't come up here will he?'

I could see her brain working, I always could. She didn't know whether to deny the black eyes and realised that she couldn't because Dot was here and very unlikely to support any of her lies. 'He will come up if he wants and you two bampots won't stop him' she said settling for not denying anything but not admitting it either.

Darlene was actually right we were all basically hypocrites; none of us had an easy time keeping our hands to ourselves including Darlene and Dorothy but were outraged when somebody else did the same.

I left the kitchen, Darlene was half cut and still drinking, it was hard enough to make any sense of what she was saying when she was sober never mind when she was drunk. As I passed through the hall David, my youngest brother was rolling up and down the hall tumbling-his-wilkies over and over.

'What are you doing you stupid eejit' I asked him.

'My ma gave me some cough medicine to take and I took it, but then I noticed it said on the bottle to shake well before use. But I forgot to shake it before I took it so I am shaking it now' he laughed like a lunatic at his stupid wee joke as did Mark and wee Tony his partners in stupidity. Charlie walked into the hall and grabbed him by the arms I quickly grabbed his legs and we shook him thoroughly until he screamed for mercy. Charlie dropped him and walked into the living room without having said a word.

'Bastards' was David's reaction, Tony and Mark thought it was funny.

'Don't think you'se three are getting drunk tonight like you'se did at Christmas, I told Charlie it was his vodka you'se drank so I would avoid him if you can' that shut the three of them up. I hadn't told Charlie anything but they didn't know that did they. They disappeared into the end room to play on the home made pool table in there. I popped my head in the living room door to make sure Patricia was alright, she was. She was sitting between my ma and Iris with a glass in her hand that probably held more than coke. So I nipped through to the pool table myself to see what was what.

There were four ten pence pieces along one of the cushions on the table and I asked whose they were.

David answered 'Paul's is first, then mine then Marks and then Tony's'

I left the first ten pence and picked up the other three and threw them to David, I then went into my pocket and put two ten pence pieces down in their place. This was the method we used to determine who was next to play on the pool table, so they had just lost their places in the queue to me and Charlie and they weren't happy.

'You canny do that' David said, as usual he was the spokesman for the three musketeers. Wee Tony probably never heard what he said with his hearing problems and Mark was too scared to say anything.

'I think you'll find that I already did, so you're wrong. Go out in the hall and finish mixing your medicine before I do, Paul will give you a shout when you're on' I said which got a laugh from Mark and Tony, but not David.

'I'll tell my da' he said

Everybody laughed at that one. 'Why is my ma busy?' I asked.

'Let him play' I heard my da said from behind me.

'I am' I said 'but he has to wait his turn, that's only fair.

'My turn was next but you through my money over to me and put yours in my place' he said with a whine in his voice.

'What's the rules here whiner?' Charlie asked as he came into the room, 'Let me remind you in case you have forgotten. We do what we want and you run greeting to my ma, we then do what we want anyway but have a good laugh at you for running greeting to my ma. So do you want your ten pence up after mine and Danny's or do you want to sit in the coal bunker with Cheeky and greet' He was referring to our cat Cheeky who used the coal bunker as her litter tray.

My da said nothing but he did smile he had six sons and he knew the same as we all did that shit runs downhill, the trick is in capturing it and throwing it back uphill when the chance presents itself and it always did, sooner or later.

'I'll put my ten pence up after you'se and when I do get on I will be taking all your money off you'se' he said with his unrealistic sense of triumph. Although in this case he was probably right, he played on this home-made table constantly and knew every wee subtle borrow and roll on it. So in truth he probably did win more games on it than anyone else. So it was a bit sad for him that when his turn to play came up we all walked out to go through to the living room as it was five to twelve and we didn't want to miss the bells. The wee sad look on his face was one that stayed with him for a while, I mean it was sad for him, it was a pleasure for us to see. He was the youngest of six brothers did he really expect an easy ride?

After the usual mad two hours following the New Year countdown Patricia and I got talking to Dot in the kitchen and she said we should come down and see her in the summer she had plenty of space and could give us a room so all we would need would be our bus or train fares. Charlie overheard this and offered to drive us down in his car it was only about three hours there and three back so he would do it in one day. We agreed and started looking forward to our first holiday. I suggested to Patricia it could be a late honeymoon.

‘We are married nearly two years you half-wit and who takes their wean on honeymoon with them you eejit’ was her ungrateful response.

‘Okay calm down, it will just be a holiday then, Patrick will love Redcar it’s got a huge beach and loads of arcades and rides along the front it’s like going to the shows’ I said.

Patricia shrugged her shoulders seemingly unimpressed, I would need to work on her, she would love it, and she just didn’t know it yet.

Darlene was well pissed by now ‘You’se can come and stay with me if you’se want, I’m not that far from Dot’s’ she slurred and then added ‘aw naw you canny actually because I will be looking after the wean’

‘You’ve got two weans Darlene not just the one’ I said.

‘Naw this wean’ she replied pointing at her stomach.

‘Are you pregnant again’ I asked.

‘Aye what about it’ she asked finishing her vodka and coke and putting her fag back in her mouth.

I looked at her and decided this was the wrong place and the wrong time to ask her why, she was blootered. Darlene being pregnant again wasn’t a great thing. Darlene was as interested in motherhood as Maggie thatcher was in Scotland. She could never understand the basics of what it meant and hated every time she had to go there. Dorothy looked at me and shrugged. Part of the reason Darlene was moving to Redcar was that every time she fell out with John Lawson she would send her daughter Charlene to stay with Dorothy in Redcar. At least if she stayed in Redcar then that would be easier. Darlene desperately needed Dorothy’s help when she was struggling. But when she thought she wasn’t struggling she resented Dot for ‘trying to steal my daughter away from me’

I was only twenty one; I didn't understand the undertones of this disagreement between my sisters. I didn't and couldn't think about whether Dorothy was trying to replace Daisy, her own daughter who died very young, or whether that was just a cruel interpretation of her trying to help Darlene in times of trouble. Dorothy had told me more than once that she would happily have adopted both of Darlene's weans if she could.

Patricia helped Darlene through to the bed in Paul's room; he had gone out at one o'clock and was unlikely to return until the morning, he was just about to turn sixteen so it was allowed. In fact it would have been a huge surprise if he hadn't gone out. What self-respecting 16 year old stays in at the bells.

I was happy enough when the time came to go back to work. I knew I would have to make a decision soon about whether I wanted to go 'on the books'. I did but it would mean less money, I had a couple of months to convince him that I was worth more than the fifteen quid a day he was paying me 'on the grip'

When I started the job it was with the purpose of identifying the worthwhile stock in two hundred pallets of stock he had bought, that turned into supervising three guys to the job and since coming back after the holidays he was putting more and more responsibility my way. He had wanted me on the books by mid-January but I kept putting him off.

One of the tasks he started putting my way was checking the lorries were loaded with the right goods before they left the yard. We supplied goods all over Scotland and it wasn't unknown for a lorry driver arriving at Aberdeen only to discover his load was for Dumfries. He wanted me to do a final check on every lorry. Seemed easy enough and it was at first, it became slightly more difficult when I discovered a pallet of nails on a lorry which didn't seem to have an address label on it. I asked the driver, he shrugged his shoulders. I asked the fork lift driver, he shrugged his shoulders. I told the driver to park up at the side until I got the rest of the lorries away and I would look into the problem.

He looked over at two of the storemen, Popeye and trumpetbum; they spotted me looking at them and quickly looked away. 'Oh shit' I thought. I had obviously stumbled on a fiddle. Popeye was cruelly given this nickname because he only had one eye, his right one being made of glass and rather skeewhiff. It took a bit of practice not to stare at his dodgy eye when talking to him. He was short and round in fact it was often joked that it was easier and quicker to jump over him than to walk round him. Trumpetbum's nickname was entirely simpler to understand he was a smelly arsed bastard who did exceptionally loud and obnoxious farts, at will. He would gleefully walk up to anyone who was concentrating on a task and let rip, scaring them with the noise and disgusting them with the smell. His favourite targets were the girls from the office believe it or not.

Whenever any of them came into the warehouse for any reason he would stalk them until he could sneak up behind them and let one rip. He never got tired of it and neither did any of the warehouse guys whenever we saw him on the prowl a hush would descend as we all watched him stalk his prey and then pounce. The girls did however get fed up with it, one even complained to the manager but he couldn't find any rules against breaking wind. She claimed it was an assault on her sense of smell and her hearing.

The manager told her it was very difficult to get concrete evidence that trumpetbum was aiming his farts directly at her. None of the warehouse staff backed up her claims that trumpetbum stalked her and aimed his arse at her. For a while the girls would only come into the warehouse in pairs. So trumpetbum gave up on the volume of sound and concentrated on what he called 'silent assassins' smelly obnoxious silent farts. He would approach the girls with a seemingly legitimate enquiry and as he was about to leave he would drop a 'Trumpet Bomb' as he also liked to call them. It was hilarious to see the girls' reaction to them, they would look at each other and then from look side to side as if looking for the source of the vileness and then scatter holding their noses and retching.

Popeye tried more than once to get trumpetbum on the telly; it was his considered opinion that trumpetbum's talent should be applauded. Hughie greens opportunity knocks didn't agree. We were outraged there were people on that show with considerably less talent than trumpetbum.

I suggested to the manager that he could get the police in and charge trumpetbum with breach of the peace; he accused me of making light of a serious situation. Things sort of came to a head when one of the office girls' boyfriends appeared at the back door one lunchtime threatening to kick trumpetbum's head in if he didn't stop annoying his bird. Popeye threatened the guy with a hammer and it could easily have got out of hand. After that he cut back on the 'trumpet bombs' the girl whose boyfriend turned up looking for a fight only stayed another month, virtually everybody shunned her. It was a shame she was a nice enough lassie but just didn't have a sense of humour; it was clearly replaced with an oversensitive sense of smell.

Trumpetbum and Popeye were both in their mid-forties and had been with this firm since before I was born. By discovering their 'fiddle' I had put myself in a delicate situation. I wanted to work here in fact I was sort of hoping for a supervisor's job, so I didn't want to be known as a grass by revealing their 'fiddle'. Equally I didn't want to let Mr McNair down, he had given me a job when I really needed one and he now wanted to take me on full time on the books. I was angry at the two idiots, three including the driver, who had put me in this position. If they had organised their fiddle properly I wouldn't have discovered it and wouldn't be in my present difficulty.

I decided that the best thing that day was to ignore it but think of some way to let them know I was on to them without creating a scene, where anything could happen. I told the driver to get on his way, much to his and his partners in crime's relief. This particular driver did what they called 'the great north run' which was actually a twice weekly trip so I had two days to think of a way of dealing with my problem. I had a brainwave after talking to Charlie, his opinion was that I should join them in the fiddle but make sure it was fool-proof first. I wasn't about to do that but it did give me an idea.

'Alistair have you got a minute?' I said to Popeye, I wasn't yet ready to call him Popeye, although he was well known by his nickname I had noticed only his best mates called him that to his face.

He looked at me with suspicion. Not only was I a casual employee who appeared to have been given some authority, I was also considered a friend of one of the bosses, Mr McNair. I wasn't a friend of his but did feel I owed him some respect.

'What's up Dan the man' Popeye eventually said.

'You know how Mr McNair gets me to check the lorries before they go out in the morning'

'Aye' he said his suspicions now on high alert, his eyes darkened. This could get ugly really quick. He knew and I knew that because I had ignored the bogus pallet a couple of days before that I had no actual evidence of any wrongdoing. He would be well within his rights to tell me to piss off if I accused him of anything.

'I was just wondering, how could I tell that a pallet wasn't legitimately on the lorry if it had an address label on it and a delivery note attached to it. Because after all the address labels and delivery notes are lying under the trade counter desk. Anybody could lift a handful of them and use them to make dodgy pallets look legit, couldn't they? So how would I know?'

He looked at me and eventually a sly grin appeared on his chops 'you wouldn'y know Dan the man, not unless you checked every delivery note and every address label against the leger in the office and if you did that it would take all day and the lorries would never get out the door.

'Aye that's what I thought' I said and walked away.

So that was that little problem sorted, I could check that all of the orders on the lorries had the correct address label for where the lorry was going. Another strange thing happened that week; I found fifty quid in my locker that I didn't remember putting there. The same thing happened almost every week for the next few months. It only stopped when I took the full time job as a warehouse supervisor and created a new system whereby the office created a drivers manifest that had to be double checked against the load on a lorry. So the potential blind-spot I had outlined to Popeye had been closed. He took it reasonably well; in fact he came up to me and shook my hand.

'Well done Dan the man, but remember there's more than one way to skin a cat' he chuckled.

'Aye there is Popeye, but there's one sure way to get sacked. Try taking the piss out of me and you will see what I mean' I grinned back. He got the message; I had got the job as supervisor in the nail section of the warehouse. There was me and three other guys that made up and despatched all customer orders for nails. No nails ever 'went missing' Popeye and trumpetbum could do what they wanted in the other sections but they didn't touch mine. I really enjoyed this job and intended keeping it.

An opportunity came along in the middle of the year for me to help my brothers out in a small way. The company I was working for had added an extra warehouse on to the side of our building. They needed people to build the pallet racking and move all the stock around. I managed to get some cash in hand weekend work for Donnie, Dunky and Charlie. Which they were glad of, Donnie and Dunky in particular as they were laid off at the time and didn't have the side-lines going the way Charlie did.

They weren't working directly under me but I saw them every day and had my dinner with them every day. During the dinner break there was usually a game of football going on in the yard which they happily joined in with. This wasn't Real Madrid versus Liverpool this was a half burst ball and players with steel toe capped boots on. Be quick or be sore was the best advice. Donnie excelled he was probably the oldest there but he still had nimble feet and ways of making opponents who tried to kick him fall on their arses. He was the master of the delicate nudge and subtle swerve; he was Cessnock's answer to Jimmy Johnstone or Willie Henderson.

He told me that he could have been a professional had he not jumped over a wall when trying to evade the police when he was about fourteen and living in Dennistoun. According to him he was running full speed away from the police and decided to jump a four foot wall to try and lose them. Unfortunately for him the wall was four foot high on the side he could see and twenty foot high on the side he couldn't see. He broke his legs in the fall and was never quite the same again. I will probably tell my grandchildren stories like that someday to explain why I never played for Scotland.

Whilst Donnie did excel in the dinner time kick-about the same can't be said for his driving skills. He for a lorry to turn up with the racking he was helping to build. I was busy unloading two lorries full of nails each lorry held twenty pallets of nails. I was zipping in and out of the back door on a fork lift lifting pallets from a lorry and depositing them straight into an appropriate space in the nail section.

I was driving what's called a reach truck; you sit side on to the direction of travel and the forks 'reach' out to enable you to lift a pallet. It's a standard type of forklift for warehouse use.

'Give me a shot of that Danny, it looks easy' Donnie said as I zipped past him heading into the warehouse with another pallet of nails for the umpteenth time, the lorries I was unloading were blocking the yard so I had to get rid of them as quickly as possible.

'Naw don't be stupid' I said as I passed him on the way back out. I didn't say anything else than that why would I, Donnie was in his thirties he wouldn't be stupid enough to jump on a forklift when nobody was looking and crash it into a wall, would he? You might expect that level of stupidity from a teenager but surely not from Donnie he was a grown man with four children'

'What the fuck are you doing Donnie' I shouted at him as I came out of the toilet block. He was hurtling towards the entrance to the warehouse on an out of control forklift.

In a way it was lucky that he missed the forty foot wide entrance into the warehouse and crashed into the wall. If he had kept the fork lift truck straight and come right into the warehouse who knows what damage he could have done. As it was the only damage he did was bruise his arse when he fell off the truck as it rebounded from the wall he hit and probably bruised his pride quite a bit as well. The truck itself was undamaged although it did have its rear wheels stuck in what looked like an old tram track.

'What did you think you were doing?' I asked him when I had stopped laughing.

'That things fucking dangerous, when you steer left it turns right' he said clearly shaken by his crash.

I could hardly stop laughing 'I know that you stupid bastard, that's the first thing I was told when I was taught to drive it. And I'll tell you something else ya numpty when you steer right it turns left. He wasn't at all amused; he somehow managed to convince himself that this was all my fault. Apparently I should have told him that if he was going to try and drive it that the steering was 'funny'. Despite the fact that I told him not to drive it, I should have known that he would try it and by not telling him about the steering it would have been my fault if he had died. I smiled at him and said 'okay' what else could I say he is my big brother.

I was actually more worried when I saw Charlie in conversation with Popeye and trumpetbum that was a combination which could only lead to disaster, disaster for me that is.

'What were you talking to them about' I asked Charlie on the way home, he was giving me a lift. I usually walked home but as he was there why not get a lift.

'A wee bit of business' he said pretending to concentrate on driving.

'Forget it; you're not doing business with them. I like this job and you're not fucking it up for me Charlie no way' I said and he knew I was serious.

'I'll keep you out of it' he said and continued looking straight ahead and avoiding looking at me.

'Stop the fucking car Charlie' I said dramatically which was a bit of a waste of time because he had arrived at my close and was stopping anyway.

'Don't get your knickers inside out Danny. It's a wee bit of business and there's no nails involved okay. Popeye told me that he stays out of your way and you stay out of his wee turns, that's a sensible arrangement and I won't spoil it' he said staring at me like he was a mafia boss.

'Charlie just shut the fuck up. If you do a turn with Popeye I'm going to kick fuck out of both of you and then sack that one eyed fat prick. How does that sound as a sensible fucking arrangement' I asked trying to imitate his stare and attitude.

'Fair enough, you don't want me shitting on your doorstep. All you had to do was tell me' he answered with his stupid grin back on his face. If he did any business with Popeye I never got to hear about it. That doesn't mean that he didn't it just means that I never got to hear about it.

It was soon summertime already and time to go and see Dorothy and Darlene in Redcar. We were going down for a couple of weeks and by a great coincidence my ma and da were going down as well for the second week we were there. So we would get a week on our own and then be joined by my ma and da and the two boys, Paul and David. Charlie iris and their two weans also decided to come down for the second week. It was going to be an invasion of McCallister's, I couldn't wait.

Charlie was driving us down to save us the bus fare, he did take a tenner for petrol but that was probably less than it was costing him. He arrived at seven in the morning desperate for a roll and sausage before we got going. We were up and waiting, Patricia obliged with the roll and sausage while I loaded our bags into the boot. There was one battered old suitcase Patrick's buggy and four 'Glendale United' kit bags. Glendale united was the local pub team I joined that year; it was as much as an excuse for a drink as for a game of football. Charlie was intrigued by the football bags.

'Who are they?' he asked.

'A football team I have started to play for'

'You're shite at football' he said with derision.

'Thanks' I said.

'You know what I mean but, you really are shite at football. You were okay at rugby but you are shite at football'

'Naw ahm no, I'm alright at football' I said, getting irritated.

'You ur shite and you know it stop lying'

'Naw I'm no, it's you that's lying'

'Can you two hear yourselves' Patricia asked 'aye am ur, naw your no'. You sound like a couple of big weans' she looked at us again and said 'my mistake, carry on, I forgot that you'se are a couple of big weans'

As Charlie drove through Glasgow to get onto the M74 and the road south I explained about Glendale.

'They are just a pub team really, the pub at the corner of Shields Road *'The Honours Three'* is sponsoring their strips this year but only two or three of the guys in the team drink in there. I have started going in for a pint before I go down the paisley road on a Tuesday and Friday' I told him.

'And a Thursday and Saturday and sometimes a Sunday' Patricia added sarcastically.

'It's no' every Saturday and Sunday it's just sometimes' I said defensively.

'When was the last Sunday that you didn'y 'go for a pint' on a Sunday after football, or instead of football when the pitch is too wet, tell me and Charlie and wee Patrick here the last time you didn'y' she said getting into her moaning stride.

I said nothing what was the point; she obviously had something to say so the easiest thing was to let her say it.

'I canny remember so why don't you tell me and Charlie and wee Patrick, you're bursting to anyway'

'The day Patrick was born that's when!' she uttered triumphantly.

'How do you know that' I said you were in hospital, 'how do you know where I went?'

'Because you told me that you went down to the masonic club with your ma and da and ended up drunk and sleeping at your ma's house, that's how I know' she said even more triumphantly.

'Did I not mention that Charlie gave me a run home to get changed and that we went into *'The honours'* for a quick one before we went to the club' I asked gleefully.

'Naw you didn'y, you're making that up. You said you went straight to the club. You told me and you're lying now to prove yourself right. You can just never be wrong Danny McCallister you're an eejit' she said and refused to answer me for the next two hours even when I admitted that I hadn't been in *'The honours'* that day.

The next time she spoke to me was on the A66 the road that takes you from the M6 across to Redcar. And she didn'y actually speak to me she screamed at me.

'Danny gonnae make him slow down he's gonnae crash'

'He's no' gonnae crash, he knows what he's doing' I don't know why I was disagreeing with her probably because of her earlier moaning. The fact was that Charlie was driving like a lunatic, but that's the way he always drove.

'I live life on the edge' he would say whenever I pulled him up about stupidity.

'You stay on the edge if you want ya bampot but drop me off first' I would reply.

The A66 is a mixture of dual carriageway and single carriageway and the road planners had maliciously made the single carriageways where the road was either hilly or bendy. Charlie liked the thrill of overtaking on a hill or round a bend; he said it tested his bottle. He tested it that day okay. He decided to overtake three lorries in a row going up a hill with a bend at the top. As we approached the top of the hill a wee blue van came tearing over the top, on the other side of the road. Which should have been okay but it wasn't because we were still on the wrong side of the road. Charlie moved left and the other driver moved right and they avoided a collision, just. The guy in the lorry behind us kept his hand on his horn for a full minute, obviously intending to let Charlie know what a dick he thought he was being.

'Slow down Charlie, my weans in the car just slow down okay' I told him, he did. But slowing down didn't stop him from overtaking. The truth was that his overtaking manoeuvres for the rest of the journey were fine and risk free, but Patricia was now so frightened that she didn't want him overtaking at all, and would scream every time he did. She failed to realise, like she always did, that screaming just encouraged him.

We got there in one piece and Dorothy as usual was working, Shirley had the keys to dot's cottage and came out with them when we pulled up outside. Shirley was Dorothy's landlady; Dorothy lived in a two bedroom cottage which was virtually at the bottom of Shirley's garden. Shirley knew both Charlie and me from when we lived with Dot for a few months some years previously. She knew Charlie better he had been back more than once I hadn't been back at all, not because I didn't like it. Just that the opportunity had never really presented itself.

'How are you boy's, have you been behaving yourselves? Well since you aren't in jail Charlie I suppose that means you have been. And who is this lovely handsome wee man?' she said.

'That's Danny' Charlie said with a laugh. Shirley had obviously been referring to Patrick and Charlie knew it.

'That's Patrick, my son, our son' I said indicating Patricia and introduced her as well.

'Well, well you are a wee cracker paddy' Shirley said to him as she held him up and gave him a kiss.

'We call him Patrick or sometimes Pat, we don't like Paddy' Patricia said softly. I wish she hadn't said that, not because of Shirley. Because of Charlie, I knew for a fact that Charlie would now never call Patrick anything else but Paddy.

'I'm sorry sweetheart Patrick it is then. Come on inside and let me make you a nice cold drink before you unpack' she offered.

'You're fine Shirley we have a couple of bottles of coke here, and anyway Patricia will need to get inside and change wee Paddy's nappy he smells worse than a miners armpit' Charlie said. I knew it I knew he would start calling him Paddy, I absolutely knew it. As soon as he came back down next week with his weans I was going to start calling his wee boy Charlie, Chas or Chazza or something, see how he liked it.

Charlie went and got his head down; he was only having a couple of hour's sleep getting something to eat and then going home again. Patricia and I unpacked our stuff and Patrick's stuff and then stood outside in Dorothy's wee bit of garden.

'We will stay in a house like this someday Danny.' She said to me wistfully 'A house with its own wee front and back door, and a wee bit of garden for the weans to play in. Someday we will Danny and I will make it lovely so I will. I would have a wee table and chairs over there and I would paint that kitchen a brighter colour, and I wouldn'y have they dark curtains in the bedroom. They would be white and the duvet covers would be white and everything would be dead bright'

'And how would you keep them white with two manky wee boys jumping all over them' Dorothy said as she appeared silently behind us. Patricia went beetroot red; I didnae mean that it wisnae nice the way it is just that...' she said before Dot interrupted her.

'I know, I know' she said laughing and then grabbed me and pulled me down for a kiss and a cuddle.

'Jesus Christ Dot. You are getting wee'er and wee'er. You have even got wee'er since Christmas. Is the gravity stronger in Redcar or something?' I asked. She slapped me on the back of my head.

'I can still reach up high enough to put your lights out' she said as she next grabbed Patrick and nuzzled him. Patricia was still a bit red and stood back a bit.

After Dot had made sure we had found the room we were to sleep in and had plenty of space to put our things she asked if we fancied a walk round town to get something for tonight's tea. When we were about to leave Charlie woke up and decided to come with us, he was intending to have a takeaway and then head back up the road. Dorothy took Patrick in the buggy so she could play with him and talk to him as much as she wanted. Dorothy adores children she really does. I think it's because she's the same height as most of them.

Patricia and Dorothy were looking in every single shop on the high street, so when Charlie suggested that we go for a couple of games of snooker and meet them back at the house. It seemed like a good idea; after all he would be heading back to Glasgow in an hour or so.

'I'm just going to stay the night on Dorothy's couch and go home tomorrow' He announced at half past eleven that night when we were both sitting on the beach steaming drunk, trying to finish our half bottle of vodka without being sick.

'Good idea' I said 'I think I might join you'

We hadn't intended getting drunk, we hadn't even intended having a drink. We had walked into the working men's club in Redcar because it had a snooker room and Charlie knew a few people in there, I ordered an orange juice and lemonade and he ordered a soda water and lime. We got a table after ten minutes and were just starting our second game when Charlie asked me. 'Do you know who that is? The old boy next to the puggie'

'Naw who is it? Remember it's years since I have been down here'

'It's Sanny Macadam' he said with a grin.

'No way, the old jakie that used to get us our carry out's' I said, Charlie just nodded and laughed.

'Christ's sake he looks almost human, what happened' I asked, honestly amazed by the transformation.

'He found himself a woman, a wee Scottish woman'

'For fuck sake wonders will never cease' I said, and then spotted somebody I did remember, Simmo.

Simmo was the ex-boyfriend of a lassie Charlie got involved with the last time we were in Redcar. We had had a few run in's with him and his nasty wee pals in fact during one of those run in's Charlie had stabbed me in the hand. Simmo also spotted us and walked straight towards us with two of his friends close behind. 'Fucking great' I thought and held my snooker cue a bit tighter.

'Charlie, you ugly wee tosser you never said you were coming down' Simmo said walking straight past me and shaking hands with Charlie.

'Just down for the day, dropping Danny and his missus off. Do you remember Danny?' Charlie said smiling at my discomfort.

'I certainly do. The comedian who likes to head butt, I never forget a face' he feinted like a boxer as if he was about to slap me or punch me. I automatically brought the pool cue up. Charlie grabbed it and said 'Calm down Danny he's only kidding you on, me and |Simmo are good mates now. Him and his missus have got a wee stall down the market here, I bring him down some sellable gear now and again, and bygones are bygones. I smiled at Simmo with my mouth not my eyes and he returned the compliment. He left after a couple of minutes but one of his wee slimy pals came back over with two pints of lager and two glasses of vodka.

It would be cheeky not to drink his drink Danny, he's just trying to be friendly' Charlie said as he downed the vodka in a one'r. That's how we started drinking and ended up pissed at half past eleven on the beach.

'What am I gonnae tell Patricia' I asked him, belatedly worrying about my wife's feelings.

'Tell her you're drunk and you're going to bed' he suggested and hiccupped.

'Very fanny' I protested and I didn't mean funny. 'She's going to do me in'

'Naw she will'ny because she knows your safe you're with me and I wouldn'y let anything happen to you. You're my big brother and I wouldn'y let anything happen to you and she knows that' he said with about as much emotion as he could manage.

'The last time we were on this beach together you stabbed me' I said by way of disputing his ability to keep me safe.

'Aye' he said 'I did, you're right I did stab you, but I wouldn'y let anybody else stab you would I, Naw I wouldn'y and she knows that and you knows that and so does she?'

It was time to head home, I was drunk but he was completely out of it now.

'I'm going for a swim' he announced.

'Naw you fuckin urny' I told him emphatically.

'Aye I fucking am' he said and started to strip off. I fought him all the way but he still managed to get naked and ran towards the water. I ran after him and rugby tackled him, getting a face full of his fat arse for my troubles. I was lying on top of him desperately trying to stop him getting up and going in the sea. I then had a sudden thought of what this would look like to anybody who might come along. I was lying on top of a naked man with my arms around him and my head pressed into his shoulder. I let him go, fuck him, let him drown if he wanted. I could always get the bus back to Glasgow.

He quickly realised that I had let him go and got on his feet and staggered towards the sea. I grabbed his clothes and followed him no longer willing to wrestle with a naked drunk. It took us ages to get to the edge of the water, Redcar has an incredibly long beach and since Charlie couldn't walk straight we were walking along the beach rather than towards the water.

'This isnae a beach this is a desert, there's no sea, where's the fuckin sea' he said and collapsed onto the sand for a rest. I sat down beside him he dragged himself over and put his head on my knee. 'Danny some bastard's stole the Pacific Ocean' was the last thing he said before he fell asleep. This was much better now I was sitting on a beach with a naked man's head in my lap, my ma would be so proud.

I managed to get him half woke up just after midnight and basically carried him home. The effort of doing that sobered me up a fair bit. The good thing was that Charlie being in such a ridiculous state and me being relatively sober gave me the chance to say to Patricia 'Gonnae look at the state of him hen, I've been following him about since seven o'clock trying to get him to stop drinking. What else could I do, I couldn'y leave him?'

She nodded her head in sympathy 'naw you couldn'y leave him, no' in that state so maybe you sleep on the couch beside him tonight. Dorothy left you'se a blanket' she said and pointed at what looked like a baby blanket on Dorothy's two seater sofa before storming out.

I quietly followed her into the bedroom and asked 'Can I not just sleep in here with you and wee Paddy' She swore at me in fact she swore a lot at me and pushed me out of the room.

I sat on the chair and looked at Charlie spread out on the couch; the bastard had laid down on it as soon as I left the room. Well he wisnae having the blanket as well, I thought and grabbed it and wrapped it around my shoulders like a shawl and fell asleep on the chair.

'My neck's all sore and that's your fault' I told Patricia as she handed me a cup of tea and some toast in the morning.

'Your neck canny be sore its made of brass' Dorothy said as she came into the room holding paddy, sorry Patrick in one arm and a cup of tea in her other hand.

'It wisnae my fault, it was fat arses fault' I said pointing at Charlie's bum cleavage which was hanging out of his trousers.

Neither of them believed me apparently. Charlie eventually woke up at two in the afternoon, phoned Iris had a cup of tea and left, Dorothy and Patricia got a kiss, I got shouted at for letting him get drunk and not telling him to phone Iris the night before. When I pointed out that he isn't very good on the phone when he is in a coma, he pointed out that there was nothing to prevent me phoning Iris and letting her know he was under the weather. I could only look at hi m open mouthed and wonder if he would ever stop blaming me.

I was in the dog house with Patricia for most of that day but the rest of that week was fantastic. Patrick was fifteen months by this time and old enough to enjoy all the wee baby rides down at the beach. The weather was fantastic and Patricia and me were either down the beach everyday with the wee man or down at the pond in Locke park. But that wasn't the best bit the best bit was when Dorothy was working and we were left in the house ourselves. This happened quite a bit we noticed that Dorothy left the house to go to work at least two hours earlier than she needed to, and it could take her a couple of hours to get home even though her house was only 500 yards from where she worked. We did see her a couple of times when we were out and about sitting in one arcade or another feeding the fruit machines. She must have been spending a fortune on them but it looked like she could afford it so it was none of our business.

We imagined it was ours and talked endlessly about what we would do to it, and how we could move here and live by the sea. I would get an office job on good money and she would get a job in one of the arcades or the café or even the bingo she had experience after all. We would get our own nice wee cottage and visit Dorothy every weekend. We could invite her ma down in the summer, even if she did have to bring Rob with her.

The shine went off the dream a wee bit when we went to visit Darlene and seen what the downside of moving to Redcar could be. Neither she nor John were working and probably because of that they weren't getting on. The house she had in Southbank wasn't great either.

John had come up to Dorothy's house to give us a lift to his and Darlene's house. He was driving a different car from the last time I had seen him but it was another convertible, he loved to be flash. It wasn't the quickest way to go but John drove along the beach road, mostly to show off and maybe to try and impress us with the number of wee lassies who waved at him and shouted 'Hi John' as if he was Paul McCartney.

It took me all my time not to say anything, Patricia kept digging me in the ribs every time she thought I was about to do so. My sides were black and blue when we got back to Dorothy's that night.

John roared into his street and slammed the brakes on at his front door, making a big entrance as usual. When we got out of the car there were four wee lassies standing at his garden gate, which was all rusty and hanging off, it matched the overgrown garden and the rubbish that was strewn about all over it. I daresay I was supposed to be impressed when he squeezed two of the lassies arses on the way past them and they both giggled. I pretended not to have noticed when he looked at me for approval.

Darlene was sitting in her living room with a cup of tea a fag and a bruise down the length of her arm. She was surrounded by dirty dishes and dirty clothes. She also had her new baby in a cot behind the couch. She had called her new baby Dorothy; she was just over a month old. That was one of the reasons my ma and da were coming down the following week, they hadn't yet seen the baby.

John followed us in to the living room and then promptly disappeared, maybe he had some teenager's arses to squeeze or something he was plainly a busy guy.

'What's up with you, look at the state of this place?' I asked, not really bothering with small talk.

'It's no' that bad, I'll tidy it up when I finish my cup of tea' she said clearly uninterested. Patricia sat down and said nothing, although I noticed her push a towel that was on the couch under her before sitting down.

Darlene's two older children came into the room, I picked Charlene up and gave her a kiss and played rough and tumble with john for a minute or two. They both ran out into the back garden to play they had piles of boxes out there that they were playing with. I followed them out and played with them for half an hour. At one point Patricia came out and told me I was immature, I told her to get out of my fort.

It wasn't my business to say anything but I said it anyway when I came back into the house. 'Are you struggling, do you want us to give you a hand to tidy up. My ma's coming down in two days; you don't want *her* to see the state of this place'

'I told you I'll tidy up when I finish my tea it will only take me ten minutes its no' that bad'

I glanced at Patricia who grimaced; she obviously thought the same as I did a team of cleaners couldn't tidy this place in a month. I hadn't seen Darlene or spoken to her since the New Year. I really didn't want to fight with her and anyway, if my ma sees this place in this state she will have a hairy canary and it will serve Darlene right. We weren't brought up in this mess and my ma won't just ignore it and say nothing. We never stayed very long and told her we wouldn't bother waiting for John to give us a lift back to town we could just walk it. I didn't realise and she didn't tell me that it was about six and a half miles. We walked a mile and then caught a bus, but I did tell her the next day that we had walked it. I think she still believes that.

Dorothy and Tony had a bit of a ding dong that night, a real plate smasher. Patricia and I basically hid in the room pretending we were asleep; Patrick spoiled that by frequently crying when voices were raised too loud. They were in the kitchen going at it hammer and tongs, it seemed to be mostly about money but some things were said that probably shouldn't have been. Particularly by Dorothy, like most McCallister's when the lid comes off her temper she has no control of where her mouth might take her.

'Patrick needs a bottle' Patricia said to me. I shrugged my shoulders.

'I'm no' going ben there listen to them two, their gonny start chibbing each other in a minute' I said to show my reluctance at getting in the middle of their fight.

'He needs fed' Patricia said defying me to deny my son food.

'Can you no' breast feed him this once' I said, I was joking but as usual she missed the joke or didn't like it.

'How stupid are you, you're supposed to have brains. I have never breast fed him. He's fifteen months old. Do you think I can just turn a switch on and make milk' she asked exasperated.

'Here that would be handy' I said 'One for milk and one for cream' and tweaked her nipples.

She went mental, and started slapping me about the head; I could hardly hear dot and Tony shouting. But then I did hear Dorothy scream and thought that was a chance to go and get the wean a bottle.

Tony did his fair share of shouting and bawling, as I stood outside the kitchen door waiting for a wee pause, he started being threatening. So I decided that was the time I should barge in and get some milk and a bottle for Patrick. It was also a reminder to Tony that I was there, I might only have been a wee boy in his eyes, but he would only make that mistake once. It wasn't just that I was concerned about Tony getting violent, he could, but so could Dot. I wouldn't really like to pick a winner between those two in a fair fight. In fact tony would win a fair fight but Dorothy wouldn't know how to fight fair.

The main reason, apart from Patrick being hungry, that I went through to the kitchen was that perhaps it would give them the opportunity of a breather. They wouldn't want to argue while I was standing there. I knew that when Patricia and I were giving it laldy we would always stop if somebody came to the door, we would start again where we left off even if it was a few hours later. Patricia's got the memory of an elephant when it comes to arguments and the memory of a goldfish when it comes to remembering when she was wrong.

My presence in the kitchen did stop them shouting for a minute but they were both still purple faced and breathless. I hoped they had been arguing and not having just having loud and rough sex to make up. They were in there thirties now so were maybe a bit past it, which would explain the purple faces and breathlessness. No of course they were still arguing. I couldn't stand there for too long or it would be too obvious. Luckily just as I was finishing filling Patrick's bottle with warm milk, Shirley, Dot's landlady came in. I wondered if she had been waiting for the shouting to stop to make her entrance the look on her face when she glanced at me told me she had.

'Dorothy I am going away to Wales at the weekend do you think your mum and dad would like to stay at my house?' she asked nervously as if Tony and Dot would start arguing about that as well. Dorothy said that would be fantastic and offered Shirley a cup of tea. Tony took the opportunity to slope off and make himself scarce or maybe to recharge his batteries for round two later on.

Shirley offering her house for the following week really was great. There had been talk about Patricia and me going to Darlene's for the week to make room for my ma and da. There was no way Dorothy was letting them stay at Darlene's, for Darlene's sake more than anything else. But if they were staying in Shirley's then we could stay where we were. A great result all round, so I made Dorothy and Shirley their cup of tea and Patricia even showed face for a cup as well having stayed in the bedroom, not having realised the fighting was over, for now. Tony and Dot didn't start fighting later on, tony came back drunk and Dot told me she really couldn't be arsed arguing with him when he was drunk. He would go from the life and soul of the party to a depressed mess in three seconds flat.

At first when he came back in he tried his old trick of carrying on with Patricia and throwing her over his shoulder and all that malarkey. She wasn't sixteen any more, she warned him to put her down and stop his shite or she would kick him in the baws. He put her down and tried to canoodle with her and then tried to lift her up on his shoulder again. She pushed him back and kicked him in the baws. She did warn him; maybe he thought she was kidding. She wasn't. He laughed it off and pretended it wasn't sore. But I knew from personal experience that it is sore, very sore.

My ma and da arrived on the Friday night near tea time in my da's old van they had brought Paul and David with them. I have no idea how that heap of shite made it to Redcar, the van I mean not wee David. Charlie Iris and their weans arrived later on that night, but not too late to go out for a drink. Paul was roped into babysitting, Charlie's two and my one. David was gleeful about this as he had plans to go down the arcades with wee Tony, but wasn't so gleeful when told he could take Tony's annoying wee brother Christopher with them and they were to be in by nine o'clock or else. Christopher was probably about nine or something and if there was one boy on earth that was more annoying than David it was Christopher. Not to me to David mostly. Christopher irritated David as much as David irritated the rest of us.

We went out to the Redcar working men's club. I was amazed there was nothing like this in Glasgow. Not that I knew off anyway, it was huge there were easily a thousand people in the hall if not more. They must have had twenty wee boys and lassies clearing the glasses off the tables alone. They had a couple of bands on the stage playing music, not at the same time of course. They also had a lassie singer and old man in his forties singing and a comedian. Who incidentally was shite; he started trying to tell stupid Scotsman jokes because he had heard a Scottish accent in the toilet before his act. The crowd let his first couple go but after his third a wee red haired guy (of course) who must have been all of five feet one, who was sat down near the stage stood up and said 'One more Scottish joke you fanny and I'm gonny thump you'

The comedian looked at the wee guy and opened his mouth, probably to say something he thought was funny to the wee guy' But before he could utter a word the curtains behind him opened and a huge big guy popped his head out and said 'and if he disnae, I'm gonny ya waarmer' It was the drummer from one of the bands who had been on earlier. The place erupted in laughter as the comedian did a double take at the big yin behind him and snapped his mouth shut. The crowd then chanted 'fight fight fight'. The big drummer waved triumphantly at the crowd trying to whip them up a bit and the comedian slipped away quietly. Me and Charlie got steaming again, every time he went to the bar I went with him to help and he bought us a wee whisky to drink while we waited for the rest of the drinks to be poured. So we got rat arsed.

'How did you no' let me go dinny skipping last week' he asked me as we sat on the wall staring into the sea.

'It's too cauld' I answered him. Patricia and the rest of them had walked on and left us to stew in our own juice and were now a couple of hundred yards ahead of us.

'But it's no' that cauld the night' I added with a mischievous grin. I was so drunk it was probably more of a grimace to be honest.

'Do you want to?' he asked with his stupit grin.

I only nodded, smiling like a madman. It took him all of ten seconds to get his gear off and he was off racing towards the sea. I shouted on my ma and da.

'Ma, da, look at that eejit, he's took all of his clothes off and he's running into the sea. He's off his bloody head' All of them came rushing back to where I stood pointing. Iris and Tony leapt down on to the sand and started chasing after Charlie. They never caught him in time because I heard the splash. Patricia came and stood beside me holding my arm, I don't know if she was holding me up or I was holding her up.

'Why are you no' in the water with him' she asked suspiciously.

'Do I look fucking daft' I said with a laugh, which would have had more impact if I hadn't stumbled and fell over the wall onto the beach at that precise moment.

I looked up at her and said 'You just let me fall that wisnae nice'

She answered 'it was between you and my new dress. You lost' and went and stood beside Dorothy who was pissing herself laughing. I don't know if she was laughing at me or at Tony and Iris trying to carry Charlie along the beach with no clothes on. Iris had taken her jacket off and tried to cover his embarrassment with it, without much success.

It was a great night and the rest of the week was brilliant as well. It was a bit of a heat-wave and we spent every day at the beach playing cricket. Dorothy worked most days but joined us at tea time. My ma absolutely loved it, I canny remember her ever being happier than that week. We had another night out in the working men's club the night before we left but it was not as good as the previous week. Probably because we were all skint by that time and had to make a pint last us for a while.

I did have a disturbing conversation with Charlie, he was sober. He told me a few weeks later he was drunk but he wasn't he was sober. It was while we were sat outside waiting for all the women to come out of the toilet in the club.

'John was trying to chat Iris up' he said softly.

'John who?' I asked.

'Darlene's man' he said.

'John wasn't even here tonight' I argued.

'No' the night, during the week' he said looking straight at me. Charlie and iris had stayed the week with Darlene and john there hadn't been space for them at Shirley's. And since Charlie had the car it was easier for him to stay there than me.

'He wouldn'y' I insisted 'he's no' that stupit'

'I know he did' Charlie said determined to make me agree.

'Did Iris tell you this' I asked, Charlie was well capable of grabbing the wrong end of any stick.

'No' exactly' He answered 'but she is being all shady about it, I know he has. He's always staring at her and trying to see down her blouse and that'

'Piss off' I said 'Don't be bloody stupit, you are forever looking down lassies tops, that disnae mean you've tried it on with all of them. In fact I've seen you looking down Patricia's top more than once'

'Don't you be stupit' he grinned 'nobody needs to look down her top she's got them out on display most of the time'

I grinned back 'if you've got it flaunt it. And she is quite proud of them anyway, and why shouldn't she be'

'Seriously but, I'm gonny sort big John out, are you up for it' he asked.

'Up for what' I asked shaking my head 'you're just about on your way home, what do you want to do? Drive over to his house and set about him with cricket bats and then we can say cheerio to Darlene and her weans before we go'

'Aye okay' he says.

'I was being sarcastic ya numpty' I said getting irritated with his stupidity. 'Just get the rest of the bags in the back of my da's van and let's go home'

He looked at me, he genuinely looked as if he was still considering fighting with John 'Alright, I'll let it go but the next time I come through here or he comes to Glasgow, if he looks at her at all, I'm going to chib him'

I told him he was mental, the thing is I am pretty sure he meant it. I travelled back up the road in my da's van, so that Patricia and Patrick could travel with Charlie, Iris and their weans. At first Patricia didn't want to in Charlie's car but I told her there was no way he would drive like a nut-job when his own weans were in the car. I was wrong and Patricia swore she would never get in a car he was driving ever again. Apart from anything else he absolutely refused to wear a seat belt even though it was made illegal not to that year. He said he could get an exemption because it gave him a pain in the neck. I said I wanted an exemption from him because he gave me a pain in the arse.

All the way back up the road my ma moaned because she hadn't had a chance to go and see Darlene's house, she reckoned that we had all conspired to keep her away from it. Which of course was true. Every time she mentioned going there Darlene would suddenly appear at Dot's or Dot would have something else planned. My ma wasn't that daft, she quizzed me all the way up the road.

'What was wrong with Darlene's house?'

'Nothing'

'Was it dirty?'

'Naw'

'Why did you'se all keep me away from it?'

‘We didnae’

‘What was she hiding?’

‘Nothing’

‘Is he hitting her?’

‘How would I know?’

‘So he was?’

‘What?’

‘You didnae say he wisnae hitting her so that means he was’

‘What?’

‘I know he was’

‘So why are you asking me if you already know?’

‘See I knew it’

‘Eh?’

‘I knew he was hitting her and you’ve just about admitted it. Did you and Charlie have a word with him? You better have, that’s your sister he’s hitting. Why did you no’ tell me while we were there instead of telling me now when I canny do anything about it. Your da would have sorted him out, I’m really angry at you for covering up for him’

‘What are you talking about ma?' I haven’t covered up for anybody. You’re making this up as you go along. Nobody says he was hitting her. I didnae say it she didnae say it Dot didnae say it, nobody said it. This is ridiculous; by the way I think Dorothy has been knocking hell out of Tony’

‘He deserves it. Tell the truth do you think John was hitting Darlene’

‘I DON’T KNOW MA’ I shouted, my head was bursting.

‘Stop shouting at your ma, I’ll stop this van and show you what shouting is about in a minute boy’ my da said, which made as much sense as anything my ma was saying, I knew what shouting was about. This relentless questioning went on for all two hundred miles from Redcar to Glasgow. In fact it felt more like two thousand miles. I even asked my da if I could go in the back of the van with David. That wee twat shouted ‘naw’ when he heard me asking. Paul wasn’t in the van because he had decided to stay on for a while in Darlene’s house. He was sixteen and I thought it wasn’t a bad idea for him to stay for a wee while. It might help him lose his virginity. Me and Charlie had spent a summer there and it didn’t do us any harm. But my ma did nothing but moan about that as well. He would get picked on by all the big English boys. It was alright for me and Charlie we had each other to rely on. Paul wasn’t as wide as us two and was easily led. Some dirty English lassie would take advantage of him. Tony would turn him into an alcoholic. He had no pals or anything down there. It was getting on my wick it really was.

I was wishing that I had made Patricia travel in the van; I would rather risk life and limb with Charlie than go through this again.

I survived the journey but one thing worried me quite a lot. The way my ma went on at me was awfully like the way Patricia went on at me. I read somewhere once that men marry their mothers and women marry their fathers. But that canny be right because both Tony and John were drunks that couldn’t keep their hands to themselves. Well maybe there was some truth in it after all.

For the rest of that year things went really well for us. I was working seven days a week and Patricia was getting more shifts at the bingo. We were probably as well off as we had been since we had got married. Christmas and the New Year were quiet for a change. We spent Christmas at our own house just me Patricia and Patrick because the wee man was nearly two and starting to know what it was about. It was great for me because I got him a train set and a ball and a wee trike. He was about eighteen months old and appeared to have started 'the terrible two's' early. He could run like the wind, glance away from him for a second and he was gone. I felt as if every day was a heart attack waiting to happen. He would struggle like mad to be put down if you tried to hold him in your arms, it was like wrestling a baby octopus. And as soon as you did he bolted, we tried one of those harness things but ended up almost strangling him he struggled to escape so much. I have no idea what we were doing to him but he seemed to spend every waking minute trying to escape from us.

I don't exactly know what happened that winter maybe it was cold or maybe the council put something in the water. But by March, believe it or not, of my ma's eight children, six of them were having children. Donnie's wife Annie was first to announce she was pregnant with her fifth wean that was just before Christmas 1983. Then Charlie announced Iris was pregnant with her third also before Christmas. Then Dunky announced Helen was expecting their second just after the New Year. Then we were all gobsmacked when we found out that Paul had got his girlfriend pregnant, which he reckoned happened at his seventeenth birthday party. And if that was a shocker, Dorothy then announced that she was pregnant as well, yes Dorothy, can you believe it? Her youngest, Christopher was coming up to ten years old, what she was thinking about having another wean now? She was thirty two for god's sake.

I think she got pregnant because of Darlene. Darlene was not a good mother and Dorothy often threatened or offered or both to take Darlene's weans off of her if she could. Buts since she couldn't do that, mainly because Darlene wouldn't let her probably needed the family allowance or something. So my guess is that when she couldn't get any of Darlene's then she just decided to have one herself, that's what I think.

The sixth and last person that year to announce a pregnancy was me, well Patricia I suppose but you know what I mean. We were having another wean and we were over the moon. We hadn't used any birth control since Patrick was born, and we were starting to wonder why she wasn't pregnant yet. I wanted a minimum of six children but wouldn't mind eight or nine, Patricia wasn't as keen she thought four would be plenty. What a year 1984 promised to be, six new weans coming and best of all one of them was ours.

Chapter Thirty; 1984 Big Brother

'You're carrying that wean all to the front, it's gonnae be a boy' my ma said to Patricia. It was July and Patricia was six months gone and quite huge, probably bigger than she was with Patrick by quite a bit.

'I think it's a lassie' Patricia responded and tried to ease herself into a chair at my ma's kitchen table. It was made more difficult by Patrick hanging on to her like a limpet. Not only was he walking now he was also talking he had turned two in March and hadn't sat down or shut up since. I was starting to regret those months teaching him to walk and talk.

'That's my baby' he said to my ma pointing at his mammy's belly.

'I know that my cheeky wee man, is it a boy or a girl' my ma asked him.

He gave her a cynical look as if to say are you daft 'No it's a baby' he answered.

He was endlessly fascinated with the bump, as we called it, whenever Patricia sat down so did he, as close to her as he could manage. He would lie with his head on her belly talking to the bump and interpreting every gurgle in her belly as an answer from the baby to him. He had entire conversations with it. Apparently it was a boy who liked coco-pops and ice cream. But he didn't like going to bed early or turnips, or his daddy farting. Which was fair enough Patricia didn't like going to bed early either, or me farting come to think of it, although she did like turnips. He didn't say hello to anybody anymore, his first words were always 'I'm going to be a big brother'.

My da came into the kitchen and picked him up and asked him 'Do you want to keep a secret for me, Paddy'

Patricia drew me a dirty look, I said 'It's Patrick da, Patricia disnae like him being called Paddy'

My da looked over his reading glasses at Patricia and said 'Okay Patty I won't call him Paddy' and went back to talking to Patrick.

'Right come and see your granda. Now put your wee hand out I'm going to give you a secret to hold and you canny show anybody it okay?' Patrick was fascinated and did as my da asked him. My da then put something in Patrick's hand and closed his fingers tightly over it.

'Now that's a secret in your hand Paddy, I mean Patrick' he frowned at Patricia again 'so don't let anybody see it okay, not even your mammy Patty'

Patrick nodded and stared at his hand for a minute or so until the temptation became too much and he opened his hand to see the secret. A sponge ball about the size of a melon bounced out of his hand, much to Patrick's delight. 'Do it again, Granda' he squealed. My da duly obliged compressing this lightweight sponge into a ball the size of a big marble. Even though the secret had been revealed Patrick wanted to do it over and over again. My ma shook her head at my da and tutted at him 'Look what you've started.

This was part of my da's new hobby, doing magic tricks. He tried them endlessly and I think maybe it was getting on my ma's nerves. In fact I know it was because every time he would try a new one out she would shout at him to grow up. He took some of them to extreme lengths. There was one night when we were all out at the Rolls Royce club at Paisley Road Toll. Dunky, Donnie and Charlie played for their snooker team, so we were all drinking there a fair bit. The snooker tables were good and the drink was cheaper than anywhere else, it was subsidised I think. I went into the toilet's looking to make room for more lager only to find my da persuading two strangers to take their shirts off and let him prepare them in such a way as he could open their collars and cuffs and whip the shirts off of them in front of everybody else when they went back to their table. It was a trick he had seen and was trying to perfect, we had all told him to beat it, and we were fed up with him either ripping buttons off our shirts or half strangling us when he tried to whip them off. He didn't appreciate it when I said to the strangers 'You can get arrested for hanging about in a gent's toilets taking your shirts off for strange men.

He also made coins which could fold and fit inside a coke bottle, the wee glass bottle I mean. He would work away at them for hours with a fret saw and tiny wee elastic bands. It was a decent enough trick when you saw it the first time by the three hundredth time when you knew how it worked it wasn't so good. To be fair the weans all loved it. The sponge ball trick was quite effective and funny he would do that to adults in pubs and since an adults hand was much bigger than Patricks it could hold six or seven of the sponge balls once they had been compressed properly. So when the man or woman, usually women, opened their hand and all these sponge balls exploded out it never failed to get a laugh. It could be done with any shape of sponge so he was forever spotting an old couch or armchair on some spare ground and he would cut it to bits with a Stanley knife. He needed an endless supply of sponges because when he showed anybody that trick in a pub he would insist on them taking the sponges home with them and trying it on their kids. He did the same with all of his tricks which was why he was forever sitting at a vice at the kitchen table sawing two pence pieces in half to make his folding coin trick. He didn't only make tricks on that vice, he also made rings. He discovered that two bob bits from before 1947 were almost entirely made of silver.

He would drill a hole in the centre and then tap tap tap away at the edges until they flattened out to form what became a silver band. I still have one of those rings and you can still see the 1942 date on it. He used to sit in the living room making these but my ma shouting at him about the incessant tap tap tap drove him into the kitchen. It would take him a couple of months to make one of these rings; I could only admire his patience.

We were all guilty of telling him his tricks were silly and childish, but it didn't stop us trying them as well. He must have made me ten of those folding coins. Charlie caught Patricia a cracker one night at my house, with a daft variation of one of the tricks. We had been out drinking and he had given me a lift home and come in to the house to use the toilet. When he was done he came into the living room where Patricia was sitting watching the television. He stood behind the armchair at the door and said 'Look at the state of the back of this chair Danny, did Patrick get a hold of a pair of scissors or a knife or something'

He then put his hand at the back of the armchair and appeared to tug at something and rip it out, when he raised his hand above the chair and opened it a huge piece of sponge erupted out of it. Patricia screamed 'that's a new suite Charlie, you better not have ripped it you bloody eejit' He had of course came in with the sponge in his hand but the look on her face was priceless.

Watching my da playing with Patrick it occurred to me how much he had changed. Perhaps it was just because I was a dad now and I was looking at things differently. I couldn't remember him playing with me the way he was playing with Patrick. In my younger mind he was a grim figure to be avoided where possible. That did change as I grew older in fact when I was about fourteen he would often take me to the golf with him. Not to play, just to walk round the course with him. Most of the time it was at Ruchhill golf course, a nine hole council run golf course just off Maryhill Road. Which wasn't the worst wee golf course in the world, but it wasn't St Andrews either. Quite a few of the neds in Maryhill used it for either off road dirt biking or as a convenient place to burn out a knocked off car. It was sometimes very difficult to putt when there was a burnt out Morris Minor in the way. He also occasionally took me to the nine hole golf course which formed part of the grounds of Leverndale hospital. Because my ma worked there as a cleaner my da was entitled to play the course. Leverndale was at the time a psychiatric hospital which it may still be to this day.

The patients were allowed to wander the course and grounds as and when they liked. It was sometimes a bit surreal to be thinking of hitting a shot into the green only for a ghostly figure in green pyjamas to wander across it. There was a regular problem at the seventh green. This was where one of the patients ran a train service to and from the ninth tee. He was, of course, not only the train but also the driver and the conductor. My da reckoned this old boy had nothing wrong with him at all. Whilst the old boy didn't charge a fare on his train, he did charge a fee of one cigarette or two roll ups to have the train stand idle for five minutes while you played your shots. And since cigarettes were as good as currency in that place the old boy was probably the equivalent of a millionaire. Charlie played with us only the once, my da wouldn't let him come back again, when he caught him lying in front of the old boy pretending to be a tree which had fallen on the track. The old boy started crying, it wasn't funny. Charlie said he wasn't crying he was just getting rid of excess water; steam trains did it all the time.

My da also taught me to play chess when I was about fourteen. Once I had got a grasp of the basics he would give me a start of maybe a bishop, a knight and a rook. As I became better that advantage was reduced until I eventually played him with a full board. I am pleased to say that although I eventually held my own with him, it wasn't a case of the pupil surpassing the master. He was a good chess player and a clever man, never to be underestimated. But the fact remains in my later teenage years and now in my early twenties he wasn't the same man as he was when I was ten. My image of him as a tyrant was no longer valid I am pleased to say. That doesn't mean that him and my ma didn't fight anymore because they most certainly did. They just didn't take it as far as they used to now.

We were down at my ma's that day for a wee tap, Patricia had stopped working when she was about five months gone. Her job in the bingo was running the floor so there was no way she could keep doing that. I thought they might have found her something else like selling the books or working behind the tea bar, but they didn't. Patricia claimed it was because the manageress in there didn't like her. I agreed she was a torn faced old woman and probably just jealous of Patricia.

I was still working and getting decent money because I was working seven days a week. But when we were both working we took too much stuff out on hire purchase. Like the suite and a new bed and a new cooker and a washing machine and a fridge and a freezer. See what I mean, far too much. So even though I was making half decent money, I got paid on a Friday and most of my wages went to the guy from the provident and the guy from Fishers. Then the rent and electric so normally we were skint by Tuesday or Wednesday. This was the first time in a long time that I had needed to ask my ma for a tap. I was nervous about asking her because she would have a go at me about having too much debt. Then she would have a go at Patricia for chucking her job too early. When she had wee David she was working up until a couple of days before going into labour.

As it turned out I didn't need to borrow any money from her, my da told me he had had a decent win on the bookies that Saturday and handed me twenty quid, which would keep us going until Friday. He then turned to Patricia and handed her twenty quid as well.

'But that's not to be spent on him or Patrick or the house, you get yourself something hen' he said. That was one good thing about my da. He was always generous particularly when he had a win at the bookies, everybody shared in his good fortune when he ever had any. That generosity also extended to people round about him when he was drinking. He would always buy the whole table a drink wherever he was, whether that was likely to be returned or not. My ma accused him of 'buying friends' when she had had a few. Which was unkind he really was just genuinely generous.

Patricia took the twenty quid and answered my da 'Okay I'll buy shoes' I had the strangest feeling of Déjà vu, I actually got goose-pimples. I looked at her and said 'I had Déjà vu there it was really weird it was as if I had heard you say exactly that before'

Then it hit me and I asked her a strange question 'Do you know where the Bellahouston Hotel is?' and she laughed.

'Why are you laughing' I asked.

'The police accused me of robbing a load of money from that hotel when I was only eight' she said.

I said nothing I knew where the strange feeling had come from. Patricia carried on with her story. 'I was out playing with my wee pal Robert, he was the same age as me, or maybe he was nine. We used to go down Maxwell park way and play about in the gardens of the big houses there. We would be careful it was one where nobody was in. Sometimes they would have had their messages delivered and they would be lying at the back door. If there were any cakes or sweeties in them we would nick them'

My ma interrupted her 'So this boy was leading you astray?'

Patricia laughed and said 'That's not how I remember it; I think it was probably the other way about. Anyway this one day we couldn't find anywhere empty to play until we came to the hotel. There was a wee flat attached to the back of it, it must have been where the manager stayed or something. We climbed over the gate at the back of the hotel just looking for mischief I suppose. There was a window open in this flat so we decided we would go and chap the door and tell who ever lived there that they had left a window open'

I interrupted her story this time 'You crafty wee besom' I said 'You'se weren't trying to help at all. You were trying to find out if anybody was in, and if there wasn't you were going in the window. You were a wee burglar, that's what you were'

She giggled again 'I canny remember if we were doing that but anyway when we chapped the door it was open. We went in shouting out hello, hello. Nobody answered' She paused to have a drink of tea; she had us all on the edge of our seats. This was so unlike her, she is as honest as the day is long. But here she was confessing to being an eight year old criminal mastermind, well almost.

'We spent hours in that wee flat; at first we were scared, well Robert was scared I was fine. But after a wee while we were treating it like our own house. We were in the fridge eating the food and drinking all the juice and some of the milk. We went into a bedroom and I was trying on women's clothes and shoes I had found in a wardrobe. And then I looked in a shoebox that was in another wardrobe and found a load of cash'

'How much' wee David asked her, he had come into the kitchen half way through her story and was as captured as we were.

'The polis said it was six hundred and eighty pounds' she said to him and smiled.

'That was a fortune back then, you shouldn't have just taken it like that' my ma said sternly.

'She was only eight ma; she would hardly know what money was' I said in Patricia's defence.

'I didnae really know it was that much Mrs McCallister but I did know it was money and I did know it was stealing' Patricia admitted, which seemed to get some kind of approval from my ma.

'So I found a handbag and we left to go home, she continued.

'But on your way out you bumped into a few young boys who were midgie raking the skip and the bins behind the hotel' I said.

'Oh I had forgot all about them, you're right there was three or four of them and the wee dark haired one said something to me' and then she looked straight at me and said 'That was you wasn't it?'

I laughed and said 'Aye it was and I remember looking in your bag and seeing all that cash and asking you what you would do with it and you said 'buy shoes' that's why I felt the Déjà vu.'

Patricia and my ma looked absolutely bewildered, what was the chance of that happening and us being married all these years later it was scary.

'So what happened to the money' David asked, it was always greed with that boy it really was.

'Oh, I gave my pal fifty quid that night and her da phoned the polis. The polis came to my ma's and got the money back. I remember a big polis with a moustache sitting me down at a table and telling me how wrong what I had done was. I just acted daft and smiled at him' Patricia said sweetly.

I shouldn't have found that cute because she does that with me all the time. Despite David's pleas to hear more about the money, I was more interested in why that seemingly insignificant incident had stayed in my mind for as long as it had. As I said I thought it was a little spooky to say the least. Something else very weird about us, but absolutely true which I discovered a fair while later. Patricia's National Security number is my date of birth. When I first saw her NI card I thought that it was normal that her number was my date of birth. We were married by then so I thought that all women had their husband's date of birth as their NI number. When Patricia told me that she had that NI number since she was sixteen then I knew what it meant. We were supposed to be together forever, it couldn't mean anything else. I mean what are the odds of that.

David poured us all a cup of tea, he had taken over the tea making duties since Paul was down in Redcar still, with his pregnant girlfriend. My ma told him to put the cake that was in the fridge on a plate and slice it so he did. The plate was passed round the table and when it came to me and Patricia there were two slices left. One slice was much bigger than the other, I looked at them and then at her and I took the bigger slice. She wasn't happy she frowned and said.

'That's quite rude you know'

'What' I asked her.

'You took the big slice of cake'

'Aye I know'

'Well if it had been me first to choose I would have taken the wee bit and left you the big bit'

I looked at her in puzzlement 'Well you've got the wee bit what are you moaning about'

My ma said I was lucky Patricia didn't hit me with the cake. See sometimes I don't understand women.

Summer rolled on there was talk of everybody going down to Redcar again but with most of them being pregnant including Dorothy. My ma said we should just leave it until next year although her and my da went down a couple of weekends when they could. They came back from one of those trips to announce that Paul was a dad he had a wee girl. That came as a major surprise to me. I had sort of lost touch with Paul when I moved up to Pollokshields. Even when I was down at Cessnock visiting my ma, it was extremely unusual for him to be in the house. Why would he be he was a teenager. But now, what seemed like a few minutes after he had left school he was a dad. What happened? I blinked and Paul grew up. I will still seeing him as the fourteen year old Teddy boy who danced with Patricia's granda at my wedding. I had been desperate to grow up but everything was going awfully fast now.

All through that summer Patricia just kept getting bigger and bigger and even more beautiful. There was something about her when she was pregnant, she was always gorgeous always. But when she was pregnant she had something else about her something magical. I could never put my finger on it, it was just something special. Which of course made me worse than a rabbit with two willies. I never gave her a minutes peace, neither I did. I even brought a book home from the library for her to read it was about having sex when you're pregnant. She ripped it up and threw the pages at me one at a time. I had to tell the library woman that I had lost it and pay a £1 fine. There was no need for that all she had to do was say no. Okay she maybe had to say it more than once. But it wasn't really fair, after all it was her that was looking the way she did, all sexy and desirable, how come that was my fault?

She told me after she was seven months gone that it wisnae safe for the baby for us to do it anymore. I didn't believe her but since she had destroyed the only book in the library that would have told me the facts, I had to accept her word. I tried to ask my ma but couldn't. I asked Iris who was also pregnant and she agreed with Patricia but she would wouldn't she, Charlie was probably the same as me or worse. He was obsessed with sex at times honestly he was. I phoned Dorothy and asked her, she said I was an ignorant selfish man and that I should leave Patricia alone. But she was six weeks further on than Patricia so that was a bit daft of me to ask her, I suppose.

When she was eight months gone in September she hardly left the house. In fact I don't think she did unless it was to go to her ma's. I know she gave up going out drinking with me early on in the summer. So when I did go out it was with my brothers and it was most Tuesdays for the darts. Then Thursday's for the snooker, I wasn't good enough for the team but I watched them and had a few games on the table that wasn't being used for matches. But I was fair to Patricia, whenever I was going out drinking I got her a puzzle book and a couple of packets of tomato sauce crisps. There you go both of us were happy it's called compromising.

With just a couple of weeks to go Patricia was big and bored and ratty, by the time she was two days overdue she was raging at it being unfair. I wanted to go and stay with my ma, both of us I mean not just me. She wasn't having it not at all, I don't know what her problem was and I don't think she did either. I was worried about Patrick and how we would manage with him if she went into labour through the night, so he was sent to stay with her ma for a couple of days just in case.

She went into labour in the middle of the night, a Thursday night, she was four days overdue. I didn't panic this time and neither did she. I went and phoned an ambulance from the phone box on the corner of the street. She stood outside the close with her vanity case, where I could see her and she could see me. When I returned she was standing bent over facing the fence at our close with both of her hands on it and breathing deeply. I stroked her back and said, 'It's okay baby, we have done this before everything's going to be fine'

She looked at me as if I had called her a name or something 'We' she said 'When did WE do this before, do you mean me? Do you mean I have done this before because I don't remember you being in labour? I don't remember you being in pain like this'

'It was quite sore when you were gripping my hand really tight during your contractions' I said trying to lighten the mood. The ambulance arrived just then, they ambulance men must have thought I was a right rotten wee shite the way she was shouting at me when they arrived. She usually had a good sense of humour as well, what is it with women? Just when you think you know them they go all mental on you.

We were up all night; her contractions were coming and going. At first I thought it was a false alarm the same as with Patrick. But it wasn't, she was having contractions, apparently they can come and go like that. By seven o'clock in the morning they had gone entirely. I went to work, there was no point in losing a day's wages and the nurse said she would phone if Patricia went into labour again.

Patricia was exhausted and was probably going to sleep all day anyway. She didn't go into labour that day, or the next day or Saturday. She was now seven days overdue and she wanted it over with. She was stressed and unhappy and I was bearing the brunt of it. I went into work on Sunday knowing that this would be the day I could feel it, and it was. I got the phone call at about eleven o'clock telling me to get to hospital Patricia was going down to theatre at one o'clock to have the baby.

I didn't think there was anything strange about that message until I got to the Southern General and Patricia was sitting up in bed with a smile on her face.

'They are coming to induce me at half eleven and I should have the baby at about one o'clock' she said.

'What does induce mean' I asked a little worriedly and sceptical, if it was that easy why di women have to go through labour why not just 'induce' weans all the time.

'It's a jag to bring on my labour, some of the women in here' she said looking round the maternity ward 'some of them say that when you are induced it shouldn't be more than an hour and a half until I have the wean'

'You know that some of the women in here talk a lot of shite don't you' I asked staring in particular at a woman opposite who had been frightening half the women in there for days with stories about still births and weans being damaged with forceps and even one wean being dropped by a nurse and ending up paralysed. If she wasn't so pregnant I would have paralysed her.

I notice a young Pakistani or Indian lassie in the bed nearest the door sitting sobbing with her weans in her arms. 'What's up with her' I whispered to Patricia.

'She's had a wee lassie' she said as if that was explanation enough for the lassie being in such a state.

'So?' I asked.

'Because she had a wee lassie her man is raging with her and her family haven't even bothered to visit her. If they don't have boys then nobody wants to know them. She's had one visitor, her sister and she told me that if it had been a boy you wouldn't have got moving in here for relatives. She said they would all have been here with gifts and food and all the rest of it but because it's a lassie, nothing'

'Well whatever you have hen I'll be happy. As long as you're alright and the wean has got all of its fingers and toes. Boy or lassie I'm fine with it' I said and kissed her forehead.

'If it's a lassie I want to call her Charlene' she said out of the blue.

'What? After Charlie do you mean?' I said surprised, she liked Charlie but not that much, he was too much of an influence on me for her to like him enough to call our wean after him.

'Naw' she said quickly 'that didn't even enter my head, you've put me off calling her that now'

'What about Margaret, after my ma or Jean after your ma' I suggested buying into the baby being a girl.

'No, Donnie's wee lassie is already called after your ma and Jean is too old fashioned, I want a modern name' she said and winced 'I had a wee twinge there I think it's starting.

'Will I get a nurse?'

'Aye go and get one'

I was ushered out to the waiting room while they made Patricia 'comfortable'. Charlie was sitting with his beaming smile on.

'Here we go again' he said 'Before you ask, Patricia's ma phoned our ma and she phoned me so here I am and ready to celebrate' He held two cigars in his hand and opened his jacket to show me the recognisable bulge of a half bottle. He didn't even smoke, he hated it, so I was guessing he had seen somebody on the telly celebrating a birth with cigars and just copied that.

'You don't even smoke'

'I know, you can have the two of them, unless Dunky turns up, I gave him a phone'

'Anybody else? Should I ask for a bigger waiting room?'

'What's up with you, ya fanny.'

'She doesn't look right, she looks no' well. They are inducing her' the blank look on his face told me he knew as much about inducing as I did. 'It means they are making her labour start up no' just letting it happen naturally' He still looked blankly at me.

'She will be fine, she's in a hospital what can go wrong?' he said without much conviction.

The nurse came back and walked me through to the labour suite, the midwife was already there and an extra midwife who looked really young. Patricia was only twenty one and this lassie looked younger than her. Patricia was sweating buckets and she looked a bit white. I stood beside her and the nurse gave me a wash cloth to wipe down Patricia's sweat. I was uncomfortable something wasn't right. When Patrick was born there was a lot of grunting and shouting but everybody in the room was happy and smiling just getting the job done.

This time I could feel a bit of hesitation in the room, it seemed to me as if they were all waiting for something to go wrong, I was starting to panic slightly. Patricia started panting like she had done with Patrick near the end.

'Just slow down Mrs McCallister' the midwife said to her. She was down at the business end looking very closely. 'Your baby is quite large so just wait until I tell you to push, do you understand'

Patricia was sweating even more which I wouldn't have thought was possible, she just nodded at the midwife's instructions, so I answered for her 'Aye she understands.'

'Mrs McCallister, I want you to hold back just for a minute or two. We need to do a little cut, just to help you so bear with us and we will get this done' The midwife said and motioned to the younger midwife to join her at the business end.

I was concentrating on soothing Patricia so if something went wrong then I didn't see it or realise. The older midwife just said 'Doctor' to the younger midwife and she was out of that room in a flash. Thirty seconds later a doctor came in and to my mind he looked anxious.

'Mr McCallister can you come with me please, your wife is a bit uncomfortable and needs the doctor to have a look at her can you come through to the waiting room please. I went with her; she had a hold of my arm so I had no real choice. I gave Patricia a kiss and wiped her head one last time. She had looked a bit pale earlier now she was as white as a ghost and her eyes were rolling. When I saw that I put up slight resistance to being pulled away from her. But the nurse was insistent and I was in a hospital, I wasn't going to start disagreeing or arguing with a nurse, they knew what was best.

'Your wife will be fine, Doctor Law is a very good doctor I promise you' she said as she left me in the waiting room with Charlie.

'Boy or a lassie?'

'Neither, she hasn't had it yet' I whispered, I could barely think let alone talk.

'We sat for half an hour, no words were spoken. I chain smoked ten fags but knocked back Charlie's offer of a drink from the half bottle. I was shaking inside and out something was wrong I could feel it. I looked at my right knee it was moving up and down and I couldn't stop it, I actually stared at it and willed my mind to tell it to stop shaking it wouldn't. I put my hand on it and physically stopped it from shaking but could still feel the vibration of it through my fingers. I was ready to burst into the labour suite and find out what was happening when the younger midwife came in and announced. 'Your wife has had a wee boy, a wee bruiser so he is nearly eight pounds' Charlie and I both stood up.

But she didn't look as happy as she should have.

'Is he okay?' Charlie asked. The nurse nodded.

'Is Patricia?' I asked. The nurse hesitated and I felt a tear escape from my eye.

'The doctor's with her he is doing everything he can'

I collapsed into the chair I had been sitting on, my mind refused to think, I was numb.

Charlie said 'What does that mean, doing all he can' the wee midwife said 'I will get somebody through to explain. But Charlie knew what it meant and so did I. Patricia was dying.

'She's gonnae die Charlie' I sobbed.

'Naw she isnae' he said and he said it with real purpose. There's no way she would leave wee paddy for you to bring up, she'll be fine'

He was always the optimist I was more realistic. I saw the look on that lassies face, I actually thought it was possible that Patricia was already gone and that wee lassie was scared to tell me. The senior midwife came into the room and sat down beside me.

'Your wife is haemorrhaging Mr McCallister, she has already lost eight pints of blood, we are giving her frequent transfusions and the doctor is with her' she said with a frown.

'She will be alright won't she' Danny said almost belligerently. 'Tell him the truth'

'She is young and strong and we are doing everything we can' she replied, but I thought she was reluctant to look me in the eye.

I couldn't say anything there was something in my throat; I think it was my heart. Charlie asked her again but more forcefully this time 'Will she be alright, gonnae tell him the truth' he now had a hitch in his voice as well.

'We are doing everything we can Mr McCallister I promise you' she said directed at me but her voice lacked the hope I needed to hear in it.

'I want to see her' I said, eventually managing to say something. She shook her head, 'That's not possible your wife is in a critical condition. I will come back and let you know of any change as soon as I can. She squeezed my hand as she stood up. I looked at Charlie and started crying in earnest. I cried for twenty minutes, Charlie said nothing he just sat beside me with one of his knees pressed against my knee and held my hand. When I pulled myself together and stopped crying like a wee baby I started pacing.

It wasn't a big waiting room probably five yards by five yards. I walked from wall to wall and back again, then from the door to the window and looked out at Corkerhill and then from the window back to the door, which I would open to see if there was any sign of the nurse coming back to tell me Patricia was dead, were they all standing over her body deciding who should tell me, is that what the delay was? I started crying as I paced how much water does your body have, how long can you cry for?

'I am going outside for a walk' I said to Charlie.

'Naw you urny' he told me emphatically. 'Patricia is going to be brand new and you need to be here when she wakes up. And you need to get a grip of that nurse and see if the weans alright'

'So I do, you're right, why has she no' showed me the wean. Is there something wrong with him Charlie is there?' The panic was rolling off me in waves, I was short of breath.

Charlie grabbed me in a bear hug and whispered in my ear 'He's fine, she's fine, you're fine' I felt one of his tears on my ear lobe, I hugged him back trying to stifle a sob. I was being such a diddy about this I couldn't believe how much of a cry baby I was being.

Another hour passed Charlie was pacing now while I was sitting, 'What the fucks keeping them. Why are they no' telling us anything?' He asked angrily. I was settling down now and trying to think clearly, surely it was good news they had been gone so long. That must mean she is still fighting and she would keep fighting I knew that. Patricia never gave in, even when she knew she was completely in the wrong she just kept fighting, she always would. The doctor came into the waiting room ten minutes later. My heart sank, it was always a doctor when it was bad news they would let the nurses tell you the good news.

'Your wife has stabilised, Mr McCallister. She is a very strong wee girl and a good fighter. You might have your work cut out with that one.' He said with the mildest of grins.

'Is she no' gonnae die/' I stupidly asked.

He smiled and said 'She will eventually but hopefully it will be in about sixty years, it certainly won't be today'

If Charlie hadn't been there standing beside me and holding me by the waist I would have fallen at the doctor's feet. As it was I was able to shake hands with him and stay on my feet. Charlie gave him a hug and a cigar, which was fine. But when he pulled the doctor down and kissed his baldy head I thought that was disrespectful and going too far.

She still looked ghostly and even her smile lacked any real strength but her eyes were open and she had the baby in her arms. He was beautiful and she was beautiful I wanted to cry again but I wouldn't. She had gone through everything for him and for me what right did I have to cry. I took a hold of the wee man and kissed his face he seemed huge, Patrick was only seven pounds so this one at eight pounds one ounce seemed huge, who would have thought a measly pound would make such a difference.

'You've got a big brother wee man, and he's gonnae love you. He's probably gonnae fight with you forever but he's gonna love you as well. It's good to have a brother son you're gonnae love it' I whispered into his ear. I looked at Patricia, she was asleep. I don't believe in god but I thanked him anyway and assured him I would be a better person from now on. I would even try out some of his commandments.

Afterword;

Thanks for joining me this far, the next part (book 6) will be include the worst time of our lives and how we cope or didn't cope with it. I hope to have it ready by the end of Feb '15 look out for it. By the way there will also be laughter; there should always be laughter, what's the point in a life with no laughter?

Printed in Great Britain
by Amazon